BOOKS BY GRAHAM GREENE

NOVELS

The Man Within
Orient Express (Stamboul Train)*
It's a Battlefield
England Made Me (The Shipwrecked)*
This Gun for Hire (A Gun for Sale)*
Brighton Rock
The Confidential Agent
The Power and the Glory
The Ministry of Fear
The Heart of the Matter
The Third Man
The End of the Affair
Loser Takes All
The Quiet American
Our Man in Havana
A Burnt-Out Case
The Comedians
Travels with My Aunt
The Honorary Consul
The Human Factor
Dr. Fischer of Geneva or The Bomb Party
Monsignor Quixote
The Tenth Man

SHORT STORIES

Twenty-One Stories
A Sense of Reality
May We Borrow Your Husband?

TRAVEL

Journey Without Maps
Another Mexico (The Lawless Roads)*
In Search of a Character

ESSAYS

Collected Essays
Graham Greene on Film (The Pleasure Dome)*
British Dramatists
J'Accuse

PLAYS

The Living Room
The Potting Shed
The Complaisant Lover
Carving a Statue
The Return of A. J. Raffles
The Great Jowett
For Whom the Bell Chimes
Yes and No

AUTOBIOGRAPHY

A Sort of Life
Ways of Escape
Getting to Know the General

BIOGRAPHY

Lord Rochester's Monkey

British title

GRAHAM GREENE

SIMON AND SCHUSTER · NEW YORK

THE
TENTH
MAN

Text copyright by MGM
Introduction and revised text copyright © 1985
by Graham Greene
All rights reserved
including the right of reproduction
in whole or in part in any form
Published by Simon and Schuster
A Division of Simon & Schuster, Inc.
Simon & Schuster Building
Rockefeller Center
1230 Avenue of the Americas
New York, New York 10020
SIMON AND SCHUSTER and colophon are
registered trademarks of Simon & Schuster, Inc.
First published in Great Britain
by The Bodley Head, Ltd., and Anthony Blond
Designed by Edith Fowler
Manufactured in the United States of America

10 9 8 7 6 5 4 3 2 1

Library of Congress Cataloging in Publication Data

Greene, Graham, date.
  The tenth man.

  1. World War, 1939–1945—Fiction. I. Title.
PR6013.R44T4 1985 823'.912 84-29830
ISBN: 0-671-50794-X

Contents

Introduction

In 1948 when I was working on *The Third Man* I seem to have completely forgotten a story called *The Tenth Man* which was ticking away like a time bomb somewhere in the archives of Metro-Goldwyn-Mayer in America.

In 1983 a stranger wrote to me from the United States telling me that a story of mine called *The Tenth Man* was being offered for sale by MGM to an American publisher. I didn't take the matter seriously. I thought that I remembered—incorrectly, as it proved— an outline which I had written toward the end of the war under a contract with my friend Ben Goetz, the representative of MGM in London. Perhaps the outline had covered two pages of typescript—there seemed, therefore, no danger of publication, especially as the story had never been filmed.

The reason I had signed the contract was that I feared when the war came to an end and I left government service that my family would be in danger from the precarious nature of my finances. I had not before

11

the war been able to support them from writing novels alone. I had indeed been in debt to my publishers until 1938, when *Brighton Rock* sold eight thousand copies and squared our accounts temporarily. *The Power and the Glory*, appearing more or less at the same time as the invasion of the West in an edition of about three thousand five hundred copies, hardly improved the situation. I had no confidence in my future as a novelist and I welcomed in 1944 what proved to be an almost slave contract with MGM which at least assured us all enough to live on for a couple of years in return for the idea of *The Tenth Man*.

Then recently came the astonishing and disquieting news that Mr. Anthony Blond had bought all the book and serial rights on the mysterious story for a quite large sum, the author's royalties of course to be paid to MGM. He courteously sent me the typescript for any revision I might wish to make and it proved to be not two pages of outline but a complete short novel of about thirty thousand words. What surprised and aggravated me most of all was that I found this forgotten story very readable—indeed I prefer it in many ways to *The Third Man*, so that I had no longer any personal excuse for opposing publication even if I had the legal power, which was highly doubtful. All the same, Mr. Blond very generously agreed to publish the story jointly with my regular publishers, The Bodley Head.

After this had been amicably arranged mystery was added to mystery. I found by accident in a cupboard in Paris an old cardboard box containing two manuscripts, one being a diary and commonplace book which I had apparently kept during 1937 and 1938. Under the date 26 December 1937 I came on this passage: "Discussed film with Menzies [an American film director]. Two notions for future films. One: a political situation like that in Spain. A decimation order. Ten men in prison draw lots with matches. A rich man draws the longest match. Offers all his money to anyone who will take his place. One, for the sake of his family, agrees. Later, when he is released, the former rich man visits anonymously the family who possess his money, he himself now with nothing but his life. . . ."

The bare bones of a story indeed. The four dots with which the entry closes seem now to represent the years of war that followed during which all memory of the slender idea was lost in the unconscious. When in 1944 I picked up the tale of Chavel and Janvier I must have thought it an idea which had just come to my mind, and yet I can only now suppose that those two characters had been working away far down in the dark cave of the unconscious while the world burned.

The unexpected return of *The Tenth Man* from the archives of MGM led also to a search in my own archives where I discovered copies of two more ideas for films, and these may amuse readers of this book. The first idea (not a bad one, it seems to me now, though nothing came of it) was called "Jim Braddon and the War Criminal."

Here is how the outline went—a not untimely story even today, with Barbie awaiting trial.

13

Jim Braddon
and the War Criminal

1

There is an old legend that somewhere in the world every man has his double. This is the strange story of Jim Braddon.

Jim Braddon was a high-grade salesman employed by a breakfast cereal company in Philadelphia: a placid honest man who would never have injured anything larger than a fly. He had a wife and two children whom he spoiled. The 1941 war had affected him little for he was over forty and his employers claimed that he was indispensable. But he took up German—he had a German grandmother—because he thought that one day this might prove useful, and that was the only new thing that happened to him between 1941 and 1945. Sometimes he saw in the paper the picture of Schreiber, the Nazi Inspector-General of the concentration camps, but except that one of his children pretended to see a likeness to this Nazi, nobody else even commented on the fact.

In the autumn of 1945 a captured U-boat com-

14

mander confessed that he had landed Schreiber on the coast of Mexico, and the film opens on a Mexican beach with a rubber dinghy upturned by the breakers and Schreiber's body visible through the thin rim of water. The tide recedes and the land crabs come out of their holes. But the hunt for Schreiber is on, for the crabs will soon eliminate all evidence of his death.

The push for postwar trade is also on, and Braddon is dispatched by his firm for a tour of Central and South America. In the plane he looks at *Life*, which carries the story of the hunt for Schreiber. His neighbor, a small, earnest, bespectacled man full of pseudo-scientific theories, points out the likeness to him. "You don't see it," he says. "I doubt whether one person in ten thousand would see it because what we mean by likeness as a rule is not the shape of the face and skull but the veil a man's experience and character throw over the features. You are like Schreiber, but no one would notice it because you have led a very different life. That can't alter the shape of the ears, but it's the expression of the eyes people look at." Apart from the joking child he is the only person who has noticed the likeness. Luckily for Braddon—and for himself—the stranger leaves the plane at the next halt. Halfway to Mexico City the plane crashes and all lives but Braddon's are lost.

Braddon has been flung clear. His left arm is broken, he is cut about the face, and he has lost his memory from the concussion. The accident has happened at night and he has cautiously—for he is a very careful man—emptied his pockets and locked his papers in his briefcase which of course is lost. When he comes to, he has no identity but his features, and those he shares with a dead man. He searches his pockets for a clue, but finds them empty of anything that will help him: only some small change, and in each pocket of the jacket a book. One is a paper-covered Heine; the other an American paperback. He finds that he can read both languages. Searching his jacket more carefully, he discovers a wad of ten-dollar notes, clean ones, sewn into the lining.

It is unnecessary in this short summary to work out his next adventures in detail: somehow he makes his way to a railroad and gets on a train to Mexico City. His idea is to find a hospital as quickly as he can, but in the washroom at the station he sees hanging by the mirror a photograph of Schreiber and a police description in Spanish and English. Perhaps the experiences of the last few days have hardened his expression, for now he can recognize the likeness. He believes he has found his name. His face takes on another expression now—that of the hunted man.

He does not know where to go or what to do: he is afraid of every policeman; he attracts attention by his furtiveness, and soon the papers bear the news that Schreiber has been seen in Mexico City. He lets his beard grow, and with the growth of the beard he loses his last likeness to the old Jim Braddon.

He is temporarily saved by Schreiber's friends, a group of Fascists to whom Schreiber had borne introductions and who are expecting him. Among these are a brother and sister—a little, sadistic, pop-eyed Mexican whom we will call Peter for his likeness to Peter Lorre and his shifty, beautiful sister whom we will call Laureen for obvious reasons of casting. Laureen sets herself the task of restoring Jim's memory—the memory which she considers Schreiber *should* possess. They fall in love: in her case without reserve, believing that she knows the worst about this man; in his with a reserve which he doesn't himself understand.

Peter, however, is incurably careless. His love of pain and violence gets in the way of caution, and as a result of some incident yet to be worked out, Jim is caught by the Mexican police, while the others escape.

Schreiber could hardly have complained of rough treatment. Nor does Jim complain. He has no memory of his crimes, but he accepts the fact that he has committed them. The police force him to sit through a film of Buchenwald, and he watches with horror and shame the lean naked victims of Schreiber. He has no longer any wish to escape. He is content to die.

He is sent north to the American authorities, and the preliminary proceedings against him start. The new bearded Schreiber face becomes a feature of the press. His family among others see the picture, but never for a moment does it occur to any of them that this is Jim.

Among the spectators at the trial, however, is the little spectacled pseudopsychologist who was on the plane with Jim. He doesn't recognize Jim, but he is puzzled by Schreiber (Schreiber is not acting true to character), and he remembers what he said to the man in the plane, that likeness is not a matter of skull measurements but of expression. The expression of horror and remorse is not one he would have expected to see in Schreiber's eyes. This man claims to have lost his

17

memory, and yet he denies nothing. Suppose after all they have got a man who is simply similar in bone structure . . .

Meanwhile Peter and Laureen, who escaped from the police trap which had closed on Jim, travel north. They plan a rescue. What their plan is I don't know myself yet. Violent and desperate, it offers one chance in a hundred. But it comes off. Jim is whipped away from the court itself, and the hunt is on again. But this is not Mexico, and the hunt is a very short one. They are trapped in a suburban villa.

But Peter has taken hostages: a woman and her child who were in the house when they broke in. Jim has been obeying his companions like an automaton: there hasn't even been time to take off his handcuffs, but at this last example of Fascist mentality his mind seems to wake. He turns on his friends and the woman he has loved. He knocks out Peter with the handcuffs and gets his gun. The woman too has a gun. They face each other across the length of the room like duelists. She says, "My dear, you won't shoot me." But he shoots and her shot comes a second after his, but it isn't aimed at him: it hits her brother, who has re-gained his feet and is on the point of attacking. Her last words are, "You aren't Schreiber. You can't be. You're decent. Who the hell are you?"

Braddon gives himself up, and the truth of the psychologist's theory is glaringly exhibited. The like-ness to Schreiber has proved to be physical only. I imagine the little man remembers at this point the man he talked to on the plane, he gives evidence, produces Braddon's family. The happy ending needs to be

18

worked out, but the strange case of Jim Braddon really comes to an end with the shots in the suburban villa. After that there's just the reaching for the coats under the seats. Anyone in the stalls could tell you what happens now.

2

The second sketch for a film, entitled *Nobody to Blame*, was written about the same time for my friend Cavalcanti. He liked the idea, but our work on it never began, for when he submitted it to the Board of Film Censors, he was told that they could not grant a certificate to a film making fun of the Secret Service. So this story too joined the others for a while in the unconscious, to emerge some ten years later as a novel—simplified but not, I think, necessarily improved—called *Our Man in Havana*.

There is no censorship for novels, but I learned later that M15 suggested to M16 that they should bring an action against the book for a breach of official secrets. What secret had I betrayed? Was it the possibility of using bird shit as a secret ink? But luckily C, the head of M16, had a better sense of humor than his colleague in M15, and he discouraged him from taking action.

19

Nobody to Blame

1

Richard Tripp is the agent of Singer Sewing Machines in some Baltic capital similar to Tallinn. He is a small inoffensive man of a rather timid disposition with a passionate love for postage stamps, Gilbert and Sullivan's works and his wife, and a passionate loyalty to Singer Sewing Machines. Unofficially he is Agent B720 of the British Secret Service. The year is 1938/39.

Mrs. Tripp—Gloria—is much younger than Tripp and it is to give her a good life that he has allowed himself to be enlisted in the Secret Service. He feels he must spend more money on her than Singer provides in order to keep her, although she has a genuine fondness for her dim husband. She knows nothing, of course, of his activities.

At HQ in London Tripp is regarded as one of their soundest agents—unimaginative, accurate, not easily ruffled. He is believed to have a network of subagents throughout Germany and he keeps in touch with HQ through the medium of his business reports written to his firm. What HQ does not know is that in fact Tripp has no agents at all. He invents all his reports and when London expresses dissatisfaction with an agent he simply dismisses one notional source and engages another equally notional. Naturally he draws salaries and expenses for all the imaginary agents.

His active imagination, from which he has drawn the details of a large underground factory near Leipzig for the construction of a secret explosive, does on one occasion lead to a little trouble with the local police. From an independent source London learns that B720 is being shadowed, and they send him an urgent warning, but the warning arrives too late.

At the end of a program of Gilbert and Sullivan opera by the Anglo-Latesthian Society in which Tripp takes a leading part, the Chief of Police, who is sitting in the front row, hands up a bouquet with a card attached and the request that he may have a drink with Tripp immediately in his dressing room. There he tells Tripp that the German Embassy have complained of his activities. Tripp confesses to his deception.

The Chief of Police is amused and pleased that Tripp's presence will keep out any serious agents, and he accepts the gift of a sewing machine for his wife. He will ensure that Tripp's messages go safely out of the country—and to keep the German Embassy quiet, he decides, they can have a look at them on the way. London's warning comes on the heels of the interview, and Tripp sends back a message announcing that he has appointed the Chief of Police himself as one of his agents, enclosing that officer's first report on the chief

21

political characters of Latesthia and requesting that as first payment and bonus the Chief, who he says is an ardent stamp collector, should receive a rare Triangular Cape, and when the stamp arrives of course he sticks it in his own album. This gives him an idea, and soon the Chief of the Secret Service is commenting to the HQ officer in charge of Tripp's station, "What a lot of stamp collectors he has among his agents."

"It might be worse. Do you remember old Stott's agents? They all wanted art photos from Paris."

"Stott's at a loose end, isn't he?"

"Yes."

"Send him over to take a look at Tripp's station. He may be able to give Tripp some advice. I always believe in letting two sound men get together."

2

Stott is a much older man than Tripp. He is bottle-nosed and mottled with a little round stomach and a roving eye. Tripp is naturally apprehensive of his visit and expects to be unmasked at any moment, but to his relief he finds that Stott is much more interested in the foods and wines of Latesthia, and in the night life, than in the details of Tripp's organization. There are even fleeting moments when Tripp wonders whether it could possibly be that Stott also had run his station on notional lines, but such a thought of course can hardly be held for long.

The first evening together Stott remarks, "Now,

the brothels, old man. You've got good contacts there, I suppose?"

Tripp has never been in a brothel in his life. He has to own that he has overlooked brothels.

"Most important, old man. Every visiting businessman goes to the brothels. Got to have them covered."

He has a night round the town with Stott and gets into trouble with his wife for returning at two in the morning. Stott moves on to Berlin, but he has sown seeds in Tripp's mind. His notional agents in future follow a Stott line. London is asked to approve in rapid succession the madame of a high class "house," a café singer, and, his most imaginative effort to date, a well-known Latesthian cinema actress who is described as Agent B720's (i.e. Tripp's) mistress. Of course he has never spoken to her in his life, and he has no idea that she is in fact a German agent.

3

A second crisis—needing more delicate handling than Stott's—blows up. The threat of European war is deepening and London considers that Tripp's position in Latesthia is a key one. He must have a proper staff: Singer Sewing Machines are persuaded in the interests of the nation to build up their agency in Latesthia and they inform Tripp that they are sending out to him a secretary-typist and a clerk. Tripp is innocently delighted that his work for Singer has borne such fruit and that sewing machines are booming. He is less pleased, however, when the clerk and typist arrive and prove to be members of the Secret Service sent to assist him in handling his now complicated network of agents.

The clerk is a young man with a penetrating cockney accent and an enormous capacity for hero worship—and heroine worship. His devotion is equally aroused by what he considers the experience and daring of Tripp and by the legs and breasts of Tripp's wife. His name is Cobb, and he has an annoying habit of asking questions. He says himself, "You don't have to bother to explain things, Chief. Just let me dig in and ask questions, and I'll get the hang of things for myself."

The typist—Miss Jixon—is a withered spinster of forty-four who regards everyone and everything with suspicion. She believes that even the most innocent laborer is in the pay of the secret police, and she is shocked by the inadequacy of the security arrangements in the office. She insists on all blotting paper being locked in the safe and all typewriter ribbons being removed at night. This is highly inconvenient as no one is very good at fixing typewriter ribbons. Once she finds a used ribbon thrown in the wastepaper basket instead of being burned in the incinerator and she begins to demonstrate the danger of the practice by deciphering the impress on the ribbon. All she can make out is "Red lips were ne'er so red nor eyes so pure," which turns out to be a line of a sonnet written by Cobb—obviously with Mrs. Tripp in mind.

"He's really rather sweet," Mrs. Tripp says.

The chief problem that Tripp has to solve is how to disguise the fact that he has no sources for his reports. He finds this unexpectedly easy. He goes shopping and returns with envelopes that have been handed to him, he says, from under the counter; he makes a great show of testing perfectly innocent letters about sewing machines for secret inks; he takes Cobb for a round of the town and now and then in the restaurants points out his agents.

"A very discreet man. You'll see he won't show the least flicker of recognition."

The monthly payments to agents present a difficulty: Miss Jixon objects strongly to the payments being made by himself.

"It's irregular, insecure: HQ would never countenance it."

By this time, for the sake of his assistants, he has drawn up an impressive chart of his sources, with the immediate head agents who control each gang. Miss Jixon insists that from now on he shall cut off his personal contacts with all but his head agents (of whom the cinema actress is one) and that he should meet them on every occasion in a different disguise.

Disguises become the bane of Tripp's life. What makes it worse, of course, is that his wife knows nothing. Miss Jixon shows a horrible ingenuity: Tripp's makeup box for the operatic productions of the Anglo-Latesthian Society is requisitioned. He finds himself being forced to slip out of back doors in red wigs and return by front doors in black wigs. She makes him carry at least two soft hats of varying colors in his overcoat pockets, so that he can change hats. Spectacles, horn-rimmed and steel-rimmed, bulge his breast pockets.

The strain tells. He becomes irritable and Mrs. Tripp is reduced to tears. Cobb is torn between hero worship and heroine worship.

4

Next crisis: the enemy begins to take Tripp seriously. He becomes aware that he is followed everywhere—even to the Anglo-Latesthian musical soirée— "an evening with Edward German and Vaughan Williams." Miss Jixon's security arrangements have been a little too good and the Germans are no longer able to keep an eye on the reports he sends.

She has objected to the use of the Chief of Police as transmitter and has evolved an elaborate method of sending secret ink messages on postage stamps. (There is a moment when Miss Jixon skirts shyly round the possibility of bird shit as a secret ink.) Unfortunately the ink never develops properly—single words will appear and disappear with disconcerting rapidity.

Tripp, in order to be able to fake his expenses sheet and show the expenditure of huge sums for entertainment, is forced to dine out at least three times a week. He hates restaurant meals—and in any case it would be fatal if one of his assistants saw him dining alone. He therefore rents a room in the suburbs and retires there for a quiet read (his favorite authors are Charles Lamb and Newbolt) or the writing of a bogus report, taking a little food out of the larder with him.

(In his account book this appears as "Dinner for three (political sources) with wines, cigars, etc., £5. 10s.0d.") This constant dining out had never been necessary in the old days before his assistants came, and Mrs. Tripp resents it.

The domestic crisis reaches its culmination when on payday Tripp has to pretend to visit the home of the cinema actress with pay for her subsources. Cobb keeps guard in the street outside and Tripp, wearing a false mustache, proceeds up to the actress's flat, rings the bell and inquires for an imaginary person. He turns away from the closing door just as Mrs. Tripp comes down from visiting a friend in the flat above. His excuse that he was trying to sell a sewing machine seems weak to Mrs. Tripp in view of his false mustache.

Domestic harmony is further shattered when Cobb, anxious to make peace between his hero and his heroine, tells Mrs. Tripp everything—or what he thinks is everything. "It's for his country, Mrs. Tripp," he says.

Mrs. Tripp decides that she too will go in for patriotism. She begins to dine out too, and Tripp, not unduly disturbed, takes the opportunity of appointing her as agent with a notional lover in the Foreign Ministry.

"That fellow Tripp," they say in London, "deserves a decoration. The Service comes even before his wife. Good show."

His notional mistress and his wife's notional lover are among his most interesting sources. Unfortunately, of course, his wife does not believe that his mistress is notional, and her dinner companion, unlike the notional member of the Foreign Ministry, is a very real young man attached to Agriculture and Fisheries.

Mrs. Tripp gets news of Tripp's hideout and decides to track him down. She is certain she will find him in the company of the actress and that he will not be engaged in work of national importance.

The enemy are aware of his hideout.

5

Tripp has got his legs up on the stove, some sausage rolls in his pocket, and he is reading his favorite poet Newbolt aloud, in a kind of subhuman drone which is his method with poetry. "Play up, play up and play the game . . . the dons on the dais serene . . ." He is surprised by a knock at the door. He opens it and is still more surprised by the sight of his notional subagent, the cinema actress. Her car has broken down outside: can she have his help? Outside in the car two thugs crouch ready to knock Tripp on the head. A third—a tall stupid sentimental-looking German of immense physique—keeps watch at the end of the street. Tripp says he knows nothing about cars; now if it had been a sewing machine . . .

Mrs. Tripp is coming up the road. She has obviously lost her way. Tripp by this time is demonstrating the special points of the Singer sewing machine . . . Mrs. Tripp is cold and miserable. She leans against a fence and cries. A little further down the road the sentimental German watches her. He is torn between pity and duty. He edges nearer.

Mr. Tripp is talking about poetry to the cinema actress . . .

Mrs. Tripp weeps on the German's shoulder and tells him how her husband is betraying her at this moment, but she can't remember the number of the house . . .

The Germans in the car are getting very cold. They get out and begin to walk up and down . . . Tripp is reading Newbolt to the actress . . . "His captain's hand on his shoulder smote . . ." Mrs. Tripp and the German peer in at the window. He hasn't realized that this treacherous husband has anything to do with him. Mrs. Tripp moans, "Take me away," and he obeys at once—in his comrades' car. Somebody—he is too sentimentally wrought up to care who—tries to stop him and he knocks him down. He deposits Mrs. Tripp at her own door.

Tripp is still reading poetry when there is another knock at the door. One German pulls in the other German who is still unconscious. There is a babble of German explanations. "He was trying to mend the car," the actress explains, "and it ran away from him."

"I'll ring up the garage," Tripp says. He goes in an alcove, where nobody has seen the telephone.

They prepare to knock him out. "Wrong number," he says furiously. "It's the police."

When he puts down the receiver again they knock him out.

6

Mr. Tripp has not returned home for some days. Cobb and Miss Jixon are worried. Mrs. Tripp is furious but finds consolation.

Tripp comes to himself inside the German Embassy. Enormous pressure is put on him to betray his organization, but he has no organization to betray. The threat forcibly resolves itself into this: either he will remain a prisoner in the Embassy until war starts, when he will be handed to the Gestapo as a spy, or he will send a message for them—containing false information carefully devised to discredit him—to London and then in due course he will be released. They show him films of concentration camps, they keep him from sleeping: he is shut up in a cell with the sentimental German, now disgraced, who wakes him whenever he tries to sleep and reproves him for betraying his wife.

The German Ambassador, in collaboration with the Military Attaché, plans out the message for him to send. On one sheet the Military Attaché notes the facts to be concealed: the date of invasion, number of divisions, etc. On the other they note the lies to be revealed. A breeze from the open window whips the papers around. The wrong notes (that is to say the true notes) are handed to Tripp to write in secret ink. Tripp gives way. To send one more message of false information seems a small price to pay.

To make all secure and ensure that no Tripp message will ever be believed again, the Germans instruct the Chief of Police to go to the British Ambassador and expose Tripp's dealings with him—the invented messages which he used to show to the Germans before transmitting them. He gives the impression that Tripp knew that the Germans saw them.

Tripp is arrested by the police immediately he leaves the German Embassy. He is escorted home where he is allowed to pack a bag. Mrs. Tripp is not there. Cobb shows him a decoded cable from London: "Dismiss Agent XY27 [his wife]. Intercepted correspondence to school friend shows she is carrying on intrigue with . . . of Agriculture and Fisheries Ministry instead of . . . of Foreign Ministry. Unreliable."

Tripp says goodbye to his home, to Cobb and Miss Jixon, to his makeup box, presented to him by the Anglo-Latesthian Society, to his collected works of Gilbert and Sullivan. He empties his pockets of the false mustache, soft hats, spectacles. "These were the trouble," he says sadly to Miss Jixon.

He is put on board a plane to England.

An official inquiry awaits him at HQ. His Ambassador's report has been received, but opinion among his judges before he comes is divided. The trouble is that his reports have been welcomed by the Armed Forces. The whole Secret Service will look foolish if they have to recall hundreds of reports over the last two years—ones which have been acclaimed as "most valuable." The head of the inquiry points out that it will discredit the whole Service. Any of their agents could have done the same. None of them will be believed in future.

A message arrives that Tripp is in the outer office, and the youngest member of the inquiry—a dapper, earnest FO type—goes out to see him. He whispers to him urgently, "Everything will be all right. Deny everything."

"If only," the chairman is saying, "he hadn't sent that last message. All his other messages are matters of opinion. You remember the underground works at Leipzig. After all, they are underground—we can't be *sure* he invented them. General Hays particularly liked that report. He said it was a model report. We've used it in our training courses. But this one—it gives a time and date for zero hour, and the source claimed—the German Military Attaché himself—you can't get round that. Such and such divisions will cross the frontiers at ten o'clock today. If we hadn't been warned by the Ambassador we'd have had the whole Army, Navy and Air Force ringing us up to know who the devil had sent such nonsense. Come in, Tripp. Sit down. This is a very serious matter. You know the charges against you."

"I admit everything."

The dapper young man whispers excitedly, "No, no, I said deny."

"You can't possibly admit everything," the chairman interrupts with equal excitement, "it's for us to tell you what you admit and what you don't admit. Of course this last message—" The telephone rings. He raises the receiver: "Yes, yes. Good God!"

He puts the receiver down and addresses the inquiry board. "The Germans crossed the Polish frontier this morning. Under the circumstances, gentlemen, I think we should congratulate Mr. Tripp on his last message from Latesthia. It is unfortunate that bun-

32

gling in the British Embassy resulted in no use being made of it—but those after all are the chances of the Service. We can say with confidence among ourselves that the Secret Service was informed of the date and time of war breaking out."

Tripp is given the OBE. He is also appointed chief lecturer at the course for recruits to the Secret Service. We see him last as he comes forward to the blackboard, cue in hand, after being introduced to the recruits as "one of our oldest and soundest officers— the man who obtained advance news of the exact date and even the hour of the German attack—Richard Tripp will lecture on 'How to Run a Station Abroad.' "

THE
TENTH
MAN

Part One

1

Most of them told the time very roughly by their
meals, which were unpunctual and irregular: they
amused themselves with the most childish games all
through the day, and when it was dark they fell asleep
by tacit consent—not waiting for a particular hour of
darkness for they had no means of telling the time exactly: in fact there were as many times as there were
prisoners. When their imprisonment started they had
three good watches among thirty-two men, and a secondhand and unreliable—or so the watch owners
claimed—alarm clock. The two wristwatches were
the first to go: their owners left the cell at seven
o'clock one morning—or seven-ten the alarm clock
said—and presently, some hours later, the watches re-
appeared on the wrists of two of the guards.

That left the alarm clock and a large old-fashioned silver watch on a chain belonging to the Mayor
of Bourge. The alarm clock belonged to an engine

driver called Pierre, and a sense of competition grew between the two men. Time, they considered, belonged to them and not to the twenty-eight other men. But there were two times, and each man defended his own with a terrible passion. It was a passion which separated them from their comrades, so that at any hour of the day they could be found in the same corner of the great concrete shed: they even took their meals together.

Once the mayor forgot to wind his watch: it had been a day of rumor, for during the night they had heard shooting from the direction of the city, just as they had heard it before the two men with wrist-watches were taken away, and the word "hostage" grew in each brain like a heavy cloud which takes by a caprice of wind and density the shape of letters. Strange ideas grow in prison and the mayor and the engine driver drew together yet more intimately; it was as though they feared that the Germans chose deliberately the men with watches to rob them of time: the mayor even began to suggest to his fellow prisoners that the two remaining timepieces should be kept hidden rather than that all should lose their services, but when he began to put this idea into words the notion suddenly seemed to resemble cowardice and he broke off in mid-sentence.

Whatever the cause that night, the mayor forgot to wind his watch. When he woke in the morning, as soon as it was light enough to see he looked at his watch. "Well," Pierre said, "what is the time? What does the antique say?" The hands stood like black neglected ruins at a quarter to one. It seemed to the mayor the most terrible moment of his life: worse, far worse, than the day the Germans fetched him. Prison leaves no sense unimpaired, and the sense of proportion is the first to go. He looked from face to face as though he had committed an act of treachery: he had surrendered the only true time. He thanked God that there was no one there from Bourge. There was a barber from Etain, three clerks, a lorry driver, a greengrocer, a tobacconist—every man in the prison but one was of a lower social plane than himself, and while he felt all the greater responsibility toward them, he also felt they were easy to deceive, and he told himself that after all it was better so: better that they should believe they still had the true time with them than trust to their unguided guesses and the secondhand alarm clock.

He made a rapid calculation by the gray light through the bars. "It's twenty-five minutes past five," he said firmly and met the gaze of the one whom he was afraid might see through his deceit: a Paris lawyer called Chavel, a lonely fellow who made awkward attempts from time to time to prove himself human. Most of the other prisoners regarded him as an oddity, even a joke—a lawyer was not somebody with whom one lived: he was a grand doll who was taken out on particular occasions, and now he had lost his black robe.

"Nonsense," Pierre said. "What's come over the antique? It's just a quarter to six."

"A cheap alarm like that always goes fast."

The lawyer said sharply as though from habit, "Yesterday you said it was slow." From that moment the mayor hated Chavel. Chavel and he were the only men of position in the prison; he told himself that never would he have let Chavel down in that way, and immediately began tortuously to seek for an explanation—some underground and disgraceful motive. Although the lawyer seldom spoke and had no friends, the mayor said to himself, "Currying popularity. He thinks he'll rule this prison. He wants to be a dictator."

"Let's have a look at the antique," Pierre said, but the watch was safely tethered by its silver chain weighted with seals and coins to the mayor's waistcoat. It couldn't be snatched. He could safely sneer at the demand.

But that day was marked permanently in the mayor's mind as one of those black days of terrible anxiety which form a private calendar: the day of his marriage; the day when his first child was born; the day of the council election; the day when his wife died. Somehow he had to set his watch going and adjust the hands to a plausible figure without anyone spotting him—and he felt the Paris lawyer's eyes on him the whole day. To wind the watch was fairly simple: even an active watch must be wound, and he had only to wind it to half its capacity, and then at some later hour of the day give it absentmindedly another turn or two.

Even that did not pass unnoticed by Pierre. "What are you at?" he asked suspiciously. "You've wound it once. Is the antique breaking down?"

"I wasn't thinking," the mayor said, but his mind had never been more active. It was much harder to find a chance to adjust the hands which for more than half the day pursued Pierre's time at a distance of five hours. Even nature could not here provide an opportunity. The lavatories were a row of buckets in the yard and for the convenience of the guards no man was allowed to go alone to a bucket: they went in parties of at least six men. Nor could the mayor wait till night, for no light was allowed in the cell and it would be too dark to see the hands. And all the time he had to keep a mental record of how time passed: when a chance occurred he must seize it, without hesitating over the correct quartering of an hour.

At last toward evening a quarrel broke out over the primitive card game—a kind of "snap" with homemade cards—that some of the men spent most of their time playing. For a moment eyes were fixed on the players and the mayor took out his watch and quickly shifted the hands.

"What is the time?" the lawyer asked. The mayor started as if he had been caught in the witness box by a sudden question: the lawyer was watching him with the strained unhappy look that was habitual to him, the look of a man who has carried nothing over from his past to buttress him in the tragic present.

"Twenty-five minutes past five."

"I had imagined it was later."

"That is my time," the mayor said sharply. It was indeed *his* time: from now on he couldn't recognize even the faintest possibility of error—his time could not be wrong because he had invented it.

2

Louis Chavel never understood why the mayor hated him. He couldn't mistake the hatred: he had seen that look too often in court on the faces of witnesses or prisoners. Now that he was himself a prisoner he found it impossible to adjust himself to the new point of view, and his tentative approaches to his fellows failed because he always thought of them as natural prisoners, who would have found themselves prisoners in any case sooner or later because of a theft, a default or a crime of sex—while he himself was a prisoner by mistake. The mayor under these circumstances was his obvious companion: he recognized that the mayor was not a natural prisoner, although he remembered clearly a case of embezzlement in the provinces in which a mayor had been concerned. He made awkward advances and he was surprised and mystified by the mayor's dislike.

The others were kind to him and friendly: they answered when he spoke to them, but the nearest they ever came to starting a conversation with him was to wish him the time of day. It seemed to him after a while terrible that he should be wished the time of day even in a prison. "Good day," they would say to him, and "Good night," as though they were calling out to him in a street as he passed along toward the courts. But they were all shut together in a concrete shed thirty-five feet long by seventeen wide.

For more than a week he had tried his best to behave like a natural prisoner, he had even forced his way into the card parties, but he had found the stakes beyond him. He would not have grudged losing money to them, but his resources—the few notes he had brought into the prison and had been allowed to keep—were beyond his companions' means, and he found the stakes for which they wished to play beyond his own. They would play for such things as a pair of socks, and the loser would thrust his naked feet into his shoes and wait for his revenge, but the lawyer was afraid to lose anything which stamped him as a gentleman, a man of position and property. He gave up playing, although in fact he had been successful and won a waistcoat with several buttons missing. Later in the dusk he gave it back to its owner, and that stamped him forever in all their eyes—he was no sportsman. They did not condemn him for that. What else could you expect of a lawyer?

No city was more crowded than their cell, and week by week Chavel learned the lesson that one can be unbearably lonely in a city. He would tell himself that every day brought the war nearer to an end—somebody must sometime be victorious and he ceased to care much who the victor was so long as an end came. He was a hostage, but it seldom occurred to him that hostages were sometimes shot. The death of his two companions only momentarily shook him: he felt too lost and abandoned to recognize the likelihood that he might himself be picked out from the crowded cell. There was safety as well as loneliness in numbers.

Once the wish to remember, to convince himself that there was an old life from which he had come and

to which he would one day return, became too acute
for silence. He shifted his place in the cell alongside
one of the clerks, a thin silent youth who was known
for some reason to his companions by the odd soubri-
quet of Janvier. Was it an unexpected touch of imagination in one of his fellow prisoners that saw him as
something young, undeveloped and nipped by the
frost?

"Janvier," Chavel asked, "have you ever trav-
eled—in France, I mean?" It was typical of the lawyer that even when he tried to make a human contact
he did so by a question as though he were addressing
a witness.

"Never been far out of Paris," Janvier said, and
then by a stretch of imagination he added, "Fontaine-
bleau. I went there one summer."

"You don't know Brinac? It's on the main line
from the Gare de l'Ouest."

"Never heard of it," the young man said sullenly,
as though he was being accused of something, and he
gave a long dry cough which sounded as though dry
peas were being turned in a pan.

"Then you wouldn't know my village, St. Jean
de Brinac? It's about two miles out of the town to the
east. That's where my house is."

"I thought you came from Paris."

"I work in Paris," the lawyer said. "When I retire
I shall retire to St. Jean. My father left me the house.
And his father left it to him."

"What was your father?" Janvier asked with
faint curiosity.

"A lawyer."

46

"And his father?"

"A lawyer too."

"I suppose it suits some people," the clerk said. "It seems a bit dusty to me."

"If you had a bit of paper," Chavel went on, "I could draw you a plan of the house and garden."

"I haven't," Janvier said. "Don't trouble anyway. It's your house. Not mine." He coughed again, pressing his bony hands down upon his knees. He seemed to be putting an end to an interview with a caller for whom he could do nothing. Nothing at all.

Chavel moved away. He came to Pierre and stopped. "Could you tell me the time?" he said.

"It's five to twelve."

From close by the mayor grunted malevolently, "Slow again."

"In your profession," Chavel said, "I expect you see the world?" It sounded like the false bonhomie of a cross-examiner who wishes to catch the witness in a falsehood.

"Yes and no," Pierre said.

"You wouldn't know by any chance a station called Brinac? About an hour's run from the Gare de l'Ouest."

"Never been on that run," Pierre said. "The Gare du Nord is my station."

"Oh, yes. Then you wouldn't know St. Jean . . ." He gave it up hopelessly, and sat down again far from anyone against the cold cement wall.

It was that night that the shooting was heard for the third time: a short burst of machine-gun fire, some stray rifle shots and once what sounded like the explosion of a grenade. The prisoners lay stretched upon the ground, making no comment to each other: they waited, not sleeping. You couldn't have told in most cases whether they felt the apprehension of men in danger or the exhilaration of people waiting beside a sickbed, listening to the first sounds of health returning to a too quiet body. Chavel lay as still as the rest. He had no fear: he was buried in this place too deeply for discovery. The mayor wrapped his arms around his watch and tried in vain to deaden the steady old-fashioned stroke: tick tock tick.

3

It was at three the next afternoon (alarm clock time) that an officer entered the cell: the first officer they had seen for weeks—and this one was very young, with inexperience even in the shape of his mustache which he had shaved too much on the left side. He was as embarrassed as a schoolboy making his first entry on a stage at a prize-giving, and he spoke abruptly so as to give the impression of a strength he did not possess. He said, "There were murders last night in the town. The aide-de-camp of the military governor, a sergeant and a girl on a bicycle." He added, "We don't complain about the girl. Frenchmen have our permission to kill Frenchwomen." He had obviously thought up his speech carefully beforehand, but the irony was overdone and the delivery that of an amateur actor: the whole scene was as unreal as a charade. He said, "You know what you are here for, living comfortably, on fine rations, while our men work and fight. Well, now you've got to pay the hotel bill. Don't blame us. Blame your own murderers. My orders are that one man in every ten shall be shot in this camp. How many of you are there?" He shouted sharply, "Number off," and sullenly they obeyed, ". . . twenty-eight, twenty-nine, thirty." They knew he knew without counting. This was just a line in his charade he couldn't sacrifice. He said, "Your allotment then is three. We are quite indifferent as to which three. You can choose for yourselves. The funeral rites will begin at seven tomorrow morning."

The charade was over: they could hear his feet striking sharply on the asphalt going away. Chavel wondered for a moment what syllable had been acted—"night," "girl," "aside," or perhaps "thirty," but it was of course the whole word—"hostage."

The silence went on a long time, and then a man called Krogh, an Alsatian, said, "Well, do we have to volunteer?"

"Rubbish," said one of the clerks, a thin elderly man in pince-nez, "nobody will volunteer. We must draw lots." He added, "Unless it is thought that we should go by ages—the oldest first."

"No, no," one of the others said, "that would be unjust."

"It's the way of nature."

"Not even the way of nature," another said. "I had a child who died when she was five . . ."

"We must draw lots," the mayor said firmly. "It is the only fair thing." He sat with his hands still pressed over his stomach, hiding his watch, but all

49

through the cell you could hear its blunt tick tock tick. He added, "On the unmarried. The married should not be included. They have responsibilities . . ."

"Ha, ha," Pierre said, "we see through that. Why should the married get off? Their work's finished. You, of course, are married?"

"I have lost my wife," the mayor said, "I am not married now. And you . . ."

"Married," Pierre said.

The mayor began to undo his watch: the discovery that his rival was safe seemed to confirm his belief that as the owner of time he was bound to be the next victim. He looked from face to face and chose Chavel—perhaps because he was the only man with a waistcoat fit to take the chain. He said, "Monsieur Chavel, I want you to hold this watch for me in case . . ."

"You had better choose someone else," Chavel said. "I am not married."

The elderly clerk spoke again. He said, "I'm married. I've got the right to speak. We are going the wrong way about all this. Everyone must draw lots. This isn't the last draw we shall have, and picture to yourselves what it will be like in this cell if we have a privileged class—the ones who are left to the end. The rest of you will soon begin to hate us. We shall be left out of your fear . . ."

"He's right," Pierre said.

The mayor refastened his watch. "Have it your own way," he said. "But if the taxes were levied like this . . ." He gave a gesture of despair.

"How do we draw?" Krogh asked.

Chavel said, "The quickest way would be to draw marked papers out of a shoe . . ."

Krogh said contemptuously, "Why the quickest way? This is the last gamble some of us will have. We may as well enjoy it. I say a coin."

"It won't work," the clerk said. "You can't get an even chance with a coin."

"The only way is to draw," the mayor said.

The clerk prepared the draw, sacrificing for it one of his letters from home. He read it rapidly for the last time, then tore it into thirty pieces. On three pieces he made a cross in pencil, and then folded each piece. "Krogh's got the biggest shoe," he said. They shuffled the pieces on the floor and then dropped them into the shoe.

"We'll draw in alphabetical order," the mayor said.

"Z first," Chavel said. His feeling of security was shaken. He wanted a drink badly. He picked at a dry piece of skin on his lip.

"As you wish," the lorry driver said. "Anybody beat Voisin? Here goes." He thrust his hand into the shoe and made careful excavations as though he had one particular scrap of paper in mind. He drew one out, opened it, and gazed at it with astonishment. He said, "This is it." He sat down and felt for a cigarette, but when he got it between his lips he forgot to light it.

Chavel was filled with a huge and shameful joy. It seemed to him that already he was saved—twenty-nine men to draw and only two marked papers left. The chances had suddenly grown in his favor from

51

ten to one to—fourteen to one: the greengrocer had drawn a slip and indicated carelessly and without pleasure that he was safe. Indeed from the first draw any mark of pleasure was taboo: one couldn't mock the condemned man by any sign of relief.

Again a dull disquiet—it couldn't yet be described as a fear—extended its empire over Chavel's chest. It was like a constriction: he found himself yawning as the sixth man drew a blank slip, and a sense of grievance nagged at his mind when the tenth man had drawn—it was the one they called Janvier—and the chances were once again the same as when the draw started. Some men drew the first slip which touched their fingers; others seemed to suspect that fate was trying to force on them a particular slip and when they had drawn one a little way from the shoe would let it drop again and choose another. Time passed with incredible slowness, and the man called Voisin sat against the wall with the unlighted cigarette in his mouth paying them no attention at all.

The chances had narrowed to one in eight when the elderly clerk—his name was Lenôtre—drew the second slip. He cleared his throat and put on his pince-nez as though he had to make sure he was not mistaken. "Ah, Monsieur Voisin," he said with a thin undecided smile, "may I join you?" This time Chavel felt no joy even though the elusive odds were back again overwhelmingly in his favor at fifteen to one: he was daunted by the courage of common men. He wanted the whole thing to be over as quickly as possible: like a game of cards which has gone on too long, he only wanted someone to make a move and break up the table. Lenôtre, sitting down against the wall next to Voisin, turned the slip over: on the back was a scrap of writing.

"Your wife?" Voisin said.

"My daughter," Lenôtre said. "Excuse me." He went over to his roll of bedding and drew out a writing pad. Then he sat down next to Voisin and began to write, carefully, without hurry, a thin legible hand. The odds were back to ten to one.

From that point the odds seemed to move toward Chavel with a dreadful inevitability: nine to one, eight to one; they were like a pointing finger. The men who were left drew more quickly and more carelessly: they seemed to Chavel to have some inner information—to know that he was the one. When his time came to draw there were only three slips left, and it appeared to Chavel a monstrous injustice that there were so few choices left for him. He drew one out of the shoe and then feeling certain that this one had been willed on him by his companions and contained the penciled cross he threw it back and snatched another.

"You looked, lawyer," one of the two men exclaimed, but the other quieted him.

"He didn't look. He's got the marked one now."

4

Lenôtre said, "Come over here, Monsieur Chavel, and sit down with us." It was as if he were inviting Chavel to come up higher, to the best table at a public dinner.

"No," Chavel said, "no." He threw the slip upon the ground and cried, "I never consented to the draw. You can't *make* me die for the rest of you . . ."

They watched him with astonishment but without enmity. He was a gentleman. They didn't judge him by their own standards: he belonged to an unaccountable class and they didn't at first even attach the idea of cowardice to his actions.

Krogh said, "Sit down and rest. There's nothing to worry about any more."

"You can't," Chavel said. "It's nonsense. The Germans won't accept me. I'm a man of property."

Lenôtre said, "Don't take on now, Monsieur Chavel. If it's not this time it's another . . ."

"You can't make me," Chavel repeated.

"It's not we who'll make you," Krogh said.

"Listen," Chavel implored them. He held out the slip of paper and they all watched him with compassionate curiosity. "I'll give a hundred thousand francs to anyone who'll take this."

He was beside himself—almost literally beside himself. It was as if some hidden calmness in him stood apart and heard his absurd proposition and watched his body take up shameful attitudes of fear and pleading. It was as if the calm Chavel whispered with ironic amusement, "A grand show. Lay it on a bit thicker. You ought to have been an actor, old man. You never know. It's a chance."

He took little rapid steps from one man to another, showing each man the bit of paper as if he were an attendant at an auction. "A hundred thousand francs," he implored, and they watched him with a kind of shocked pity: he was the only rich man among them and this was a unique situation. They had no means of comparison and assumed that this was a characteristic of his class, just as a traveler stepping off the liner at a foreign port for luncheon sums up a nation's character forever in the wily businessman who happens to share the table with him.

"A hundred thousand francs," he pleaded, and the calm shameless Chavel at his side whispered, "You are getting monotonous. Why haggle? Why not offer them everything you possess?"

"Calm yourself, Monsieur Chavel," Lenôtre said. "Just think a moment—no one is going to give his life for money he'll never enjoy."

"I'll give you everything I've got," Chavel said, his voice breaking with despair, "money, land, everything, St. Jean de Brinac . . ."

Voisin said impatiently, "None of us want to die, Monsieur Chavel," and Lenôtre repeated with what seemed to the hysterical Chavel shocking self-righteousness, "Calm yourself, Monsieur Chavel."

Chavel's voice suddenly gave out. "Everything," he said.

They were becoming impatient with him at last. Tolerance is a question of patience, and patience is a question of nerves, and their nerves were strained. "Sit down," Krogh rapped at him, "and shut your mouth." Even then Lenôtre made a friendly space for him, patting the floor at his side.

"Over," the calm Chavel whispered, "over. You

weren't good enough. You've got to think up something else . . ."

A voice said, "Tell me more. Maybe I'll buy." It was Janvier.

5

He never really expected an offer: hysteria and not hope had dictated his behavior, and now it took him a long moment to realize that he was not being mocked. He repeated, "Everything I've got." The hysteria peeled off like a scab and left the sense of shame.

"Don't laugh at him," Lenôtre said.

"I'm not laughing. I tell you I'll buy."

There was a long pause as though no one knew what to do next. How does one hand over everything one possesses? They watched him as though they expected him to empty his pockets. Chavel said, "You'll take my place?"

"I'll take your place."

Krogh said impatiently, "What'll be the good of his money then?"

"I can make a will, can't I?"

Voisin suddenly took the unlighted cigarette out of his mouth and dashed it to the floor. He exclaimed, "I don't like all this fuss. Why can't things go natural? We can't buy *our* lives, Lenôtre and me. Why should he?"

Lenôtre said, "Calm yourself, Monsieur Voisin."

"It's not fair," Voisin said.

Voisin's feeling was obviously shared by most of

the men in the cell. They had been patient with Chavel's hysteria—after all it's no joke to be a dying man and you couldn't expect a gentleman to behave quite like other people: that class were all, when you came down to it, a bit soft perhaps—but this that was happening now was different. As Voisin said, it wasn't fair. Only Lenôtre took it calmly: he had spent a lifetime in business and he had watched from his stool many a business deal concluded in which the best man did not win.

Janvier interrupted. "Fair?" he said. "Why isn't it fair to let me do what I want? You'd all be rich men if you could, but you haven't the spunk. I see my chance and I take it. Fair, of course it's fair. I'm going to die a rich man and anyone who thinks it isn't fair can rot." The peas rolled again on the pan as he coughed. He quelled all opposition: already he had the manner of one who owned half the world. Their standards were shifting like great weights—the man who had been rich was already halfway to being one of themselves and Janvier's head was already lost in the mists and obscurity of wealth. He commanded sharply, "Come here. Sit down here." And Chavel obeyed, moving a little bent under the shame of his success.

"Now," Janvier said, "you're a lawyer. You've got to draw things up in their proper form. How much money is there?"

"Three hundred thousand francs. I can't tell you exactly."

"And this place you were talking about? St. Jean."

"Six acres and a house."

57

"Freehold?"

"Yes."

"And where do you live in Paris? Have you got a house there?"

"Only a flat. I don't own that."

"The furniture?"

"No—books only."

"Sit down," Janvier said. "You make me out— what's it called?—a deed of gift."

"Yes. But I want paper."

"You can have my pad," Lenôtre said.

Chavel sat beside Janvier and began to write: "I, Jean-Louis Chavel, lawyer, of Rue Miromesnil 119, Paris, and St. Jean de Brinac . . . all stocks and shares, money to my account at . . . all furniture, movables . . . the freehold property at St. Jean de Brinac . . ." He said, "It will need two witnesses," and Lenôtre immediately from force of habit offered himself, coming forward as it were from the outer office just as though his employer had rung a bell and called him in.

"Not you," Janvier said rudely. "I want living men as witnesses."

"Would you perhaps?" Chavel asked the mayor as humbly as if it were he who were the clerk.

"This is a very odd document," the mayor said. "I don't know that a man in my position ought to sign . . ."

"Then I will," Pierre said and splashed his signature below Chavel's.

The mayor said, "Better have someone reliable. That man would sign anything for a drink," and he squeezed his own signature in the space above Pierre's.

As he bent they could hear the great watch in his pocket ticking out the short time left before dark.

"And now, the will," Janvier said. "You put it down—everything I've got to my mother and sister in equal shares."

Chavel said, "That's simple: it only needs a few lines."

"No, no," Janvier said, "put it down again there . . . the stocks and shares and money in the bank, the freehold property . . . they'll want something to show the neighbors at home what sort of a man I am." When it was finished Krogh and the greengrocer signed. "You keep the documents," Janvier told the mayor. "The Germans may let you send them off when they've finished with me. Otherwise you've got to keep them till the war ends . . ." He coughed, leaning back with an air of exhaustion against the wall. He said, "I'm a rich man. I always knew I'd be rich."

The light moved steadily away from the cell; it rolled up like a carpet from one end to the other. The dusk eliminated Janvier while the clerk sitting by Voisin could still find light enough to write by. A grim peace descended, the hysteria was over and there was no more to be said. The watch and the alarm clock marched out of step toward night, and sometimes Janvier coughed. When it was quite dark Janvier said, "Chavel." It was as if he was calling a servant and Chavel obeyed. Janvier said, "Tell me about my house."

"It's about two miles out of the village."

"How many rooms?"

"There is the living room, my study, the drawing room, five bedrooms, the office where I interview people on business, of course bathroom, kitchen . . . the servants' room."

"Tell me about the kitchen."

"I don't know much about the kitchen. It's a large one, stone paved. My housekeeper was always satisfied."

"Where's she?"

"There's no one there. When the war came I shut the house up. I was lucky. The Germans never hit on it."

"And the garden?"

"There's a little terrace above a lawn: the grounds slope and you can see all the way to the river, and beyond that St. Jean . . ."

"Did you grow plenty of vegetables?"

"Yes, and fruit trees: apple, plum, walnut. And a greenhouse." He continued as much to himself as to Janvier: "You don't see the house when you enter the garden. There's a wooden gate and a long curving gravel drive with trees and shrubs. Suddenly it comes right out in front of the terrace, and then divides: the left-hand path leads off to the servants' quarters, and the right round to the front door. My mother used to keep a lookout for visitors she didn't want to meet. Nobody could call without her seeing him arrive. My grandfather, when he was young, used to watch in just the same way as my mother . . ."

"How old's the house?" Janvier interrupted.

"Two hundred and twenty-three years old," Chavel said.

"Too old," Janvier said. "I'd have liked something modern. The old woman has rheumatics."

The darkness had long enclosed them both and now the last light slid off the ceiling of the cell. Men automatically turned to sleep. Pillows like children were shaken and slapped and embraced. Philosophers say that past, present and future exist simultaneously, and certainly in this heavy darkness many pasts came to life: a lorry drove up the Boulevard Montparnasse, a girl held out her mouth to be kissed, and a town council elected a mayor; and in the minds of three men the future stood as inalterably as birth—fifty yards of cinder track and a brick wall chipped and pitted.

It seemed to Chavel now his hysteria was over that that simple track was infinitely more desirable after all than the long obscure route on which his own feet were planted.

Part Two

6

A man calling himself Jean-Louis Charlot came up the drive of the house at St. Jean de Brinac.

Everything was the same as he had remembered it and yet very slightly changed, as if the place and he had grown older at different rates. Four years ago he had shut the house up, and while for him time had almost stood still, here time had raced ahead. For hundreds of years the house had grown older almost imperceptibly: years were little more than a changed shadow on the brickwork. Like an elderly woman the house had been kept in flower—the face lifted at the right moment. Now in four years all that work had been undone: the lines broke through the enamel which had not been renewed.

In the drive the gravel was obscured by weeds; a tree had fallen right across the way, and though somebody had lopped the branches for firewood, the trunk still lay there to prove that for many seasons no car had driven up to the house. Every step was familiar to the bearded man who came cautiously round every bend like a stranger. He had been born here: as a child he had played games of hide-and-seek in the bushes; as a boy he had carried the melancholy and sweetness of first love up and down the shaded drive. Ten yards further on there would be a small gate onto the path which led between heavy laurels to the kitchen garden.

The gate had gone: only the posts showed that memory hadn't failed him. Even the nails which had held the hinges had been carefully extracted to be used elsewhere for some more urgent purpose. He turned off the drive. He didn't want to face the house yet: like a criminal who returns to the scene of his crime or a lover who returns to haunt the place of farewell he moved in intersecting circles; he didn't dare to move in a straight line and finish his pilgrimage prematurely, with nothing more to do forever after.

The greenhouse had obviously been unused for years, though he remembered telling the old man who worked in the garden that he was to keep the garden stocked, and sell the vegetables for what he could get in Brinac. Perhaps the old man had died and no one in the village had the initiative to appoint himself as successor. Perhaps there was no one left in the village. From the trampled unsown earth beside the greenhouse he could see the ugly red-brick church pointing like an exclamation mark at the sky, closing a sentence he couldn't read from here.

Then he saw that something after all had been planted: a patch had been cleared of weeds for the sake of some potatoes, cabbages, savoys. It was like the garden you give to children to cultivate: a space little larger than a carpet. All around the desolation lapped.

He remembered what had been here in the old days—
the strawberry beds, the bushes of currants and rasp-
berries, the sweet and bitter smell of herbs. The wall
which separated this garden from the fields had tum-
bled in one place, or else some looter had picked his
way through the old stonework to get into the garden:
it had all happened a long time ago, for nettles had
grown up over the fallen stones. From the gap he
stood and looked a long time at something which had
been beyond the power of time to change, the long
slope of grass toward the elms and the river. He had
thought that home was something one possessed, but
the things one had possessed were cursed with change;
it was what one didn't possess that remained the same
and welcomed him. This landscape was not *his*, not
anybody's home: it was simply home.

Now there was nothing more for him to do except go away. If he went away, what could he do but
drown himself in the river? His money was nearly
gone: already after less than a week of liberty he had
learned how impossible it was for him to find work.

At seven o'clock in the morning (five minutes
past by the mayor's watch and two minutes to by
Pierre's alarm clock) the Germans had come for Voisin, Lenôtre and Janvier. That had been his worst
shame up to date, sitting against the wall, watching his
companions' faces, waiting for the crack of the shots.
He was one of them now, a man without money or
position, and unconsciously they had accepted him,
and begun to judge him by their own standards, and to
condemn him. The shame he felt now shuffling like a
beggar up to the door of the house went nearly as

deep. He had realized reluctantly that Janvier could still be used for his benefit even after his death.

The empty windows watched him come like the eyes of men sitting round the wall of a cell. He looked up once and took it all in: the unpainted frames, the broken glass in what had been his study, the balustrade of the terrace broken in two places. Then his eyes fell to his feet again, scuffling up the gravel. It occurred to him that the house might still be empty, but when he turned the corner of the terrace and came slowly up the steps to the door, he saw the same diminutive signs of occupation as he had noticed in the kitchen garden. The steps were spotless. When he put out his hand and pulled the bell it was like a gesture of despair. He had tried his best not to return but here he was.

7

The flags of rejoicing had been months old when Jean-Louis Charlot had come back to Paris. The uppers of his shoes were still good, but the soles were nearly paper thin, and his dark lawyer's suit bore the marks of many months' imprisonment. He had thought of himself in the cells as a man who kept up appearances, but now the cruel sun fingered his clothes like a secondhand dealer, pointing out the rubbed cloth, the missing buttons, the general dinginess. It was some comfort that Paris itself was dingy too.

In his pocket Charlot had a razor wrapped in a bit of newspaper with what was left of a tablet of soap, and he had three hundred francs. He had no papers, but he had something which was better than papers—the slip from the prison officer in which the Germans had carefully recorded a year before the incorrect details he had given them—including the name Charlot. In France at this moment such a document was of more value than legal papers, for no collaborator possessed a German prison dossier authenticated with most efficient photographs, full face and profile. The face had altered somewhat, since Charlot had grown his beard, but it was still, if carefully examined, the same face. The Germans were thoroughly up-to-date archivists: photographs can be easily substituted on documents, plastic surgery can add or eliminate scars; but it is not so simple to alter the actual measurements of the skull, and these the Germans had documented with great thoroughness.

Nevertheless no collaborator felt a more hunted man than Charlot, for his past was equally shameful: he could explain to no one how he had lost his money—if indeed it was not already known. He was haunted at street corners by the gaze from faintly familiar faces and driven out of buses by backs he imagined he knew: deliberately he moved into a Paris that was strange to him. His Paris had always been a small Paris: its arc had been drawn to include his flat, the law courts, the Opéra, the Gare de l'Ouest and one or two restaurants—between these points he knew only the shortest route. Now he had but to sidestep and he was in unknown territory: the Metro lay like a jungle below him; Combat and the outer districts were deserts through which he could wander in safety.

But he had to do more than wander: he had to get

a job. There were moments—after his first glass of wine in freedom—when he felt quite capable of beginning over again: of re-amassing the money he had signed away; and finally in a burst of daydream he had bought back his home at St. Jean de Brinac and was wandering happily from room to room when he saw the reflection of his face—Charlot's bearded face—in the water decanter. It was the face of failure. It was odd, he thought, that one failure of nerve had ingrained the face as deeply as a tramp's, but, of course, he had the objectivity to tell himself, it wasn't one failure, it was a whole lifetime of preparation for the event. An artist paints his picture not in a few hours but in all the years of experience before he takes up the brush, and it is the same with failure. It was his good fortune to have been a fashionable lawyer: he had inherited more money than he had ever earned; if it had depended upon himself he would never, he believed now, have reached the heights he had.

All the same, he now made several attempts to earn his living in a reasonable way. He applied for the post of a teacher at one of the innumerable language institutes in the city. Although the war still muttered outside the borders of France, the Berlitzes and kindred organizations were already doing a thriving trade: there were plenty of foreign soldiers anxious to learn French to take the place of peacetime tourists.

He was interviewed by a dapper thin man in a frock coat which smelled very faintly of mothballs. "I'm afraid," he said at length, "your accent is not good enough."

"Not good enough!" Charlot exclaimed.

"Not good enough for this institute. We exact a very high standard. Our teachers must have the best, the very best, of Parisian accents. I am sorry, monsieur." He enunciated himself with terrible clarity, as though he was used to speaking only to foreigners, and he used only the simplest phrases—he was trained in the direct method. His eyes dwelt ruminatively on Charlot's battered shoes. Charlot went.

Perhaps something about the man reminded him of Lenôtre. It occurred to him immediately he had left the institute that he might earn a reasonably good living as a clerk: his knowledge of law would be useful, and he could explain it by saying that at one time he had hoped to be called to the bar, but his money had given out . . .

He answered an advertisement in *Figaro:* the address was on the third floor of a high gray building off the Boulevard Haussmann. The office into which he found his way gave the impression of having been just cleaned up after enemy occupation: dust and straw had been swept against the walls and the furniture looked as though it had been recently uncrated from the boxes in which it had been stored away ages ago. When a war ends one forgets how much older oneself and the world have become: it needs something like a piece of furniture or a woman's hat to waken the sense of time. This furniture was all of tubular steel, giving the room the appearance of an engine room in a ship, but this was a ship which had been beached for years—the tubes were tarnished. Out of fashion in 1939, in 1944 they had the air of period pieces. An old man greeted Charlot: when the furniture was new he must have been young enough to have an eye for the fashionable, the chic, for appearances. He sat down among the steel chairs at random as though he was in a public waiting room and said sadly, "I suppose like everyone else you have forgotten everything?"

"Oh," Charlot said, "I remember enough."

"We can't pay much here at present," the old man said, "but when things get back to normal . . . there was always a great demand for our product . . ."

"I would begin," Charlot said, "at a low salary . . ."

"The great thing," the old man said, "is enthusiasm, to believe in what we are selling. After all, our product has proved itself. Before the war our figures were very good, very good indeed. Of course, there was a season, but in Paris there are always foreign visitors. And even the provinces bought our product. I'd show you our figures, only our books are lost." From his manner you would have thought he was attracting an investor rather than interviewing a would-be employee.

"Yes," Charlot said, "yes."

"We've got to make our product known again. When once it's known, it can't fail to be as popular as before. Craftsmanship tells."

"I expect you are right."

"So you see," the old man said, "we've all got to put our backs into it . . . a cooperative enterprise . . . the sense of loyalty . . . your savings will be quite safe." He waved his hand above the wilderness of tubular chairs. "I promise you that."

Charlot never learned what the product was, but on the landing below a wooden crate had been opened and standing in the straw was a table lamp about three feet high built hideously in steel in the shape of the Eiffel Tower. The wire ran down the lift shaft like the rope of an ancient hotel lift, and the bulb screwed in on the top floor. Perhaps it was the only table lamp the old man had been able to obtain in Paris: perhaps—who knows?—it may have been the product itself . . .

Three hundred francs wouldn't last long in Paris. Charlot answered one more advertisement, but the employer demanded proper papers. He was not impressed by the prison dossier. "You can buy any number of those," he said, "for a hundred francs," and he refused to be persuaded by the elaborate measurements of the German authorities. "It's not my job to measure your skull," he said, "or feel your bumps. Go off to the city hall and get proper papers. You seem a capable fellow. I'll keep the job open until noon tomorrow . . ." But Charlot did not return.

He hadn't eaten more than a couple of rolls for thirty-six hours: it suddenly occurred to him that he was back exactly where he had started. He leaned against a wall in the late afternoon sun and imagined that he heard the ticking of the mayor's watch. He had come a long way and taken a deal of trouble and was back at the end of the cinder track with his back against the wall. He was going to die and he might just as well have died rich and saved everybody trouble. He began to walk toward the Seine.

Presently he couldn't hear the mayor's watch any more: instead there was a shuffle and pad whichever way he turned. He heard it just as he had heard the mayor's watch and he half realized that both were delusions. At the end of a long empty street the river shone. He found that he was out of breath and he leaned against a urinal and waited for a while with his head hanging down because the river dazzled his eyes. The shuffle and pad came softly up behind him and stopped. Well, the watch had stopped too. He refused to pay attention to delusion.

"Pidot," a voice said, "Pidot." He looked sharply up, but there was no one there.

"It is Pidot, surely?" the voice said.

"Where are you?" Charlot asked.

"Here, of course." There was a pause and then the voice said like conscience almost in his ear, "You look all in, finished. I hardly recognized you. Tell me, is anyone coming?"

"No." In childhood, in the country, in the woods behind Brinac one had believed that voices might suddenly speak out of the horns of flowers or from the roots of trees, but in the city when one had reached the age of death one couldn't believe in voices from paving stones. He asked again, "Where are you?" and then realized his own dull-wittedness—he could see the legs from the shins downward under the green cape of the urinal. They were black pin-striped trousers, the trousers of a lawyer or a doctor or even a deputy, but the shoes hadn't been cleaned for some days.

"It's Monsieur Carosse, Pidot."

"Yes?"

74

"You know how it is. One's misunderstood."

"Yes."

"What could I have done? After all, I had to keep the show going. My behavior was strictly correct—and distant. No one knows better than you, poor Pidot. I suppose they are holding things against you too?"

"I'm finished."

"Courage, Pidot. Never say die. A second cousin of mine who was in London is doing his best to put things right. Surely you know one of them?"

"Why don't you come out from there and let me see you?"

"Better not, Pidot. Separately we might pass muster, but together . . . it's too risky." The pinstriped trousers moved uneasily. "Anyone coming, Pidot?"

"No one."

"Listen, Pidot. I want you to take a message to Madame Carosse. Tell her I'm well: I've gone south. I shall try to get into Switzerland till it all blows over. Poor Pidot, you could do with a couple of hundred francs, couldn't you?"

"Yes."

"I'll leave them on a ledge in here. You'll take the message, won't you, Pidot?"

"Where to?"

"Oh, the same old place. You know—on the third floor. I hope the old lady's still got her hair. The old bitch was proud of it. Well, goodbye and good luck, Pidot." There was a scuffle in the urinal, and then the

shuffle and pad went off in the other direction. Charlot watched the stranger go: tall and stout and black-
clothed, with a limp and the kind of hat Charlot himself would have worn—so many years ago—between
the Rue Miromesnil and the law courts.

On a shelf of the urinal there was a screw of
paper—three hundred francs. Whoever Monsieur
Carosse was, he had the rare virtue of being better
than his word. Charlot laughed: the sound was hollow
among the metal alcoves. A week had gone by and he
was back exactly where he had started with three hundred francs. It was as if all that time he had lived upon
air—or rather as if some outwardly friendly but inwardly malign witch had granted him the boon of an
inexhaustible purse, but a purse from which he could
never draw more than three hundred francs. Was it
perhaps that the dead man had allocated him this allowance out of his three hundred thousand?

We'll soon test that out, Charlot thought; what's
the good of making this last a week and be only a
week older and a week shabbier at the end of it? It was
the hour of apéritifs and for the first time since he had
entered Paris, he deliberately stepped into his own
territory, the territory of which he knew every yard.

He had not until then properly appreciated the
strangeness of Paris: an unfamiliar street might always
have been an unfrequented one, but now he noticed
the emptiness, the silent little bicycle taxis gliding by,
the shabbiness of awnings and the strange faces. Only
here and there he saw the familiar face of the customary stranger sitting where he had sat for years, sipping
the same drink. They were like the remains of an old

flower garden sticking up in a wilderness of weeds after a careless tenant's departure.

I am going to die tonight, Charlot thought: what does it matter if someone does recognize me? And he pushed through the glass door of his accustomed café and made for the very corner—the right-hand end of the long sofa under the gilt mirror—in which he had always sat as a kind of right. It was occupied.

An American soldier sat there: a young man with high cheekbones and a rough puppy innocence; and the waiter bowed and smiled and exchanged words with him as though he were the oldest customer in the place. Charlot sat and watched: it was like an act of adultery. The headwaiter, who had always stopped for a word, went past him as though he did not exist, and he too paused by the American's table. The explanation soon came—the big bundle of notes the Yankee produced to pay with—and suddenly it occurred to Charlot that he too formerly had possessed a big bundle of notes, had been a payer; it wasn't that he was a ghost now: he was merely a man without much money. He drank his brandy and called for another: the slowness of the service angered him. He called the headwaiter. The man tried to avoid him but at last he had to come.

"Well, Jules," Charlot said.

The shallow eyes flickered disapproval: the man only liked his intimates—the payers, Charlot thought—to call him by his name.

"You don't remember me, Jules," Charlot said.

The man became uneasy: perhaps some tone of voice echoed in his ear. The times were confusing:

some customers had disappeared altogether, others who had been in hiding had returned changed by imprisonment, and others who had not been in hiding it was now in the interests of his business to discourage. "Well, monsieur, you have not been here for some time . . ."

The American began to hit loudly on the table with a coin. "Excuse me," the waiter said.

"No, no, Jules, you can't leave an old customer like that. Leave out the beard." He laid his hand across his chin. "Can't you see a fellow called Chavel, Jules?"

The American beat again with his coin, but this time Jules paid him no attention, simply signaled another waiter across to take the man's order. "Why, Monsieur Chavel," he said, "you are so much changed. I'm astonished . . . I heard . . ." But it was obvious that he couldn't remember what he had heard. It was difficult to remember which of his customers were heroes and which traitors and which simply customers.

"The Germans locked me up," Chavel said.

"Ah, that must have been it," Jules said with relief. "Paris is nearly itself again now, Monsieur Chavel."

"Not quite, Jules." He nodded at his old place.

"Ah, I'll see that seat is kept for you tomorrow, Monsieur Chavel. How is your house—where was it?"

"Brinac. There are tenants there now."

"It hasn't suffered?"

"I don't think so. I haven't visited it yet. To tell you the truth, Jules, I only arrived in Paris today. I've barely enough money for a bed."

"I can accommodate you a little, Monsieur Chavel?"

"No, no. I shall manage somehow."

"At least you must be our guest this evening. Another cognac, Monsieur Chavel?"

"Thank you, Jules." The test, he thought, has worked: the pocketbook is inexhaustible. I still have my three hundred francs.

"Do you believe in the Devil, Jules?"

"Naturally, Monsieur Chavel."

He was moved to recklessness. "You hadn't heard, Jules, that I am selling Brinac?"

"Are you getting a good price, Monsieur Chavel?"

Suddenly Charlot felt a great distaste for Jules: it seemed to him incredible that a man could be so crass. Had he no possession in the world for which a good price was an insufficient inducement? He was a man who would sell his life . . . He said, "I'm sorry."

"What for, Monsieur Chavel?"

"After these years haven't we all reason to be sorry for a hundred things?"

"We have no reason to be sorry here, Monsieur Chavel. I assure you our attitude has always been strictly correct. I have always made a point of serving Frenchmen first—yes, even if the German was a general."

He envied Jules: to have been able to remain "correct": to have saved his self-respect by small doses of rudeness or inattention. But for him—to have remained correct would have meant death. He said suddenly, "Do you know if any trains are running yet from the Gare de l'Ouest?"

"A few and they are very slow. They haven't got

the fuel. They stop at every station. Sometimes they stop all night. You wouldn't get to Brinac before morning."

"There's no hurry."

"Are they expecting you, Monsieur Chavel?"

"Who?"

"Your tenants."

"No." The unaccustomed brandy was running along the dry subterranean channels of his mind: sitting there in the familiar café, where even the mirrors and cornices were chipped in the places he remembered, he felt an enormous longing just to be able to get up and catch a train and go home as he had often done in past years. Suddenly and unexpectedly to give way to a whim and find a welcome at the other end. He thought: After all, there is always time in which to die.

8

The bell like most things about the place was old-fashioned. His father had disliked electricity, and though he could well have afforded to bring it to Brinac, he had preferred oil lamps almost until his death (saying they were better for the eyes) and ancient bells which dangled on long fronds of metal. Himself he had loved the place too much to change things: when he came down to Brinac it was to a quiet cave of dusk and silence—no telephone could petulantly pursue him there. So now he could hear the long twanging wire before the bell began to swing at the back of the house, in the room next to the kitchen. Surely if he had been in the house that bell would have had a different tone: one less hollow, more friendly, less sporadic, like a cough in a worn-out breast . . . A cold early-morning breeze blew through the bushes and stirred at ankle level the weeds in the drive: somewhere—perhaps in the potting shed—a loose board flapped. Without warning the door opened.

This was Janvier's sister. He recognized the type and in a flash built her up on the lines of her brother. Fair and thin and very young she had still had time to develop what must have been the family trait of recklessness. Now that he was here and she was there, he found he had no words of explanation: he stood like a page of type waiting to be read.

"You want a meal," she said. She had read the whole page like so many women do at a glance, even to the footnote of his thin shoes. He made a gesture which might have been deprecation or acceptance. She said, "We haven't much in the house. You know how things are. It would be easier to give you money."

He said, "I've got money . . . three hundred francs."

She said, "You'd better come in. Make as little dirt as you can. I've been scrubbing these steps."

"I'll take off my shoes," he said humbly, and he followed her in, feeling the parquet floor cold under his socks. Everything had changed a little for the worse. There was no question but that the house had been surrendered to strangers: the big mirror had been taken down and left an ugly patch on the wall; the tallboy had been shifted, a chair had gone; the steel

81

engraving of a naval engagement off Brest had been hung in a new place—tastelessly he thought. He looked in vain for a photograph of his father, and exclaimed suddenly, furiously, "Where's . . . ?"

"Where's what?"

He checked himself. "Your mother," he said.

She turned round and looked at him as though she had missed something on the first reading. "How do you know about my mother?"

"Janvier told me."

"Who's Janvier? I don't know any Janvier."

"Your brother," he said. "We used to call your brother that in the prison."

"You were with him there?"

"Yes."

He was to learn in time that she never quite did the expected thing: he had imagined that now she would call her mother, but instead she laid her hand on his arm and said, "Don't speak so loud." She explained, "My mother doesn't know."

"About his death?"

"About anything. She thinks he's made a fortune—somewhere. Sometimes it's England, sometimes South America. She says she always knew he was a clever son. What's your name?"

"Charlot. Jean-Louis Charlot."

"Did you know the other one too?"

"You mean . . . Yes, I knew him. I think I'd better go before your mother comes."

A high old voice cried from the stairs, "Thérèse, who's that you've got?"

"Somebody," the girl said, "who knows Michel."

An old woman heaved herself down the last stairs into the hall, a huge old woman draped in shawl after shawl until she appeared like an unturned bed: even the feet were swathed, they padded and slopped toward him. It was difficult to see pathos in this mountain or appreciate the need to shelter her. Surely these huge maternal breasts were there to comfort, not to require comfort. "Well," she said, "how's Michel?"

"He's well," the girl said.

"I didn't ask you. You. How did you leave my son?"

"He was well," Charlot repeated. "He asked me to look you up and see how you were."

"He did, did he? He might have given you a pair of shoes to come in," she said sharply. "He hasn't done anything foolish, has he, lost his money again?"

"No. No."

"He bought all this for his old mother," she went on with fond fanaticism. "He's a foolish boy. I was all right where I was. We had three rooms in Menilmontant. Manageable they were, but here you can't get help. It's too much for an old woman and a girl. He sent us money too, of course, but he doesn't realize there's things nowadays money won't buy."

"He's hungry," the girl interrupted.

"All right, then," the old woman said. "Give him food. You'd think he was a beggar the way he stands there. If he wants food why doesn't he ask for food?" she went on just as though he were out of earshot.

"I'll pay," Charlot snapped at her.

"Oh, you'll pay, will you? You're too ready with your money. You won't get anywhere that way. You don't want to offer money till you're asked for it." She was like an old weatherworn emblem of wisdom—something you find in desert places, like the Sphinx—and yet inside her was that enormous vacancy of ignorance which cast a doubt on all her wisdom.

One turned out of the hall on the left, through a door with a chipped handle. This led to a long stone passage leading halfway round the house: he remembered in winter how the food was never quite hot after its journey from the kitchen and how his father had always planned alterations, but in the end the house had won. Now without thinking he took a step toward the door as though he would find his own way there: then stopped and thought, I must be careful, so careful. He followed silently behind Thérèse and thought how odd it was to see someone young in that house where he only remembered old, trustworthy, crusty servants. Only in portraits were people young: the photograph in the best bedroom of his mother on her wedding day, of his father when he had taken his degree in law, his grandmother with her first child. Following the girl he thought with melancholy that it was as if he had brought a bride to the old house.

She gave him bread and cheese and a glass of wine and sat down opposite him at the kitchen table. He was silent because of his hunger and because of his thoughts. He had hardly been in the kitchen since he was a child: then he would come in from the garden about eleven and see what he could scrounge. There was an old cook—old again—who loved him and fed him and gave him odd toys to play with—he could remember only a potato forked like a man, a merrythought dressed carefully up as an old woman in a bonnet, and a mutton bone which he believed then was like an assegai.

The girl said, "Tell me about him." It was what he had dreaded, arming himself with suitable false phrases. He said, "He was the life and soul of the prison—even the guards liked him."

She interrupted him: "I didn't mean Michel . . . I mean the other one."

"The man who . . ."

"I mean Chavel," she said. "You don't think I'd forget his name, do you? I can see it just as he wrote it on the documents. Jean-Louis Chavel. Do you know what I tell myself? I tell myself that one day he will come back here because he won't be able to resist seeing what's happened to his beautiful house. We have lots of strangers passing through here like yourself, hungry, but every time that bell starts swinging, I think to myself, 'Maybe it's him.' "

"And then?" Charlot said.

"I'd spit in his face," she said, and for the first time he noticed the shape of her mouth: a beautiful mouth as he remembered Janvier's had been. "That's the first thing I'd do . . ."

He watched it when he said, "All the same, it's a lovely house."

"Sometimes," she said, "if it wasn't for the old woman I think I'd set it alight. What a fool he was," she cried out at Charlot as though this was the first time she had had a chance of saying what she thought aloud. "Did he really think I'd rather have this than him?"

"You were twins, weren't you?" Charlot said, watching her.

"Do you know the night they shot him I felt the pain? I sat up in bed crying . . ."

"It wasn't at night," Charlot said, "it was in the morning."

"Not in the night?"

"No."

"What did it mean then?"

"Just nothing," Charlot said. He began to cut a bit of cheese into tiny squares. "That's often the way. We think there's a meaning but then we find the facts are wrong—there just isn't one. You wake with a pain and afterwards you think that was love—but the facts don't fit."

She said, "We loved each other so much. I feel dead too."

He cut the cheese and cut the cheese. He said gently, "The facts are wrong. You'll see." He wanted to convince himself that he wasn't responsible for two deaths. He felt thankful that it was in the night that she had woken and not in the morning, at seven o'clock.

"You haven't told me," she said, "what *he* looks like."

He chose his words with great care. "He's a little taller than I am—perhaps an inch, or not so much. He's a clean shaven . . ."

"That doesn't mean a thing," she said. "You can grow a beard in a week. What color eyes?"

"Blue. They looked gray in some lights, though."

"Can't you think of a single thing you can tell

him by for certain? Hasn't he got a scar somewhere?"

He was tempted to lie but resisted: "No," he said. "I can't remember anything like that about him. He was just a man like the rest of us."

"I thought once," the girl said, "that I'd have someone from the village here to help us and to keep an eye out for him. But I wouldn't trust one of them. He was popular there. I suppose because they'd known him from when he was a kid. You don't trouble about a kid's meanness, and by the time he's grown up, you're so used to it, you don't notice." She had her wise sayings as her mother had, but hers had not been inherited: they had been learned in the street with her brother; they had an odd masculine tinge.

"Do they know down there," he asked, "what he's done?"

"It wouldn't make any difference if they did. He'd have just put a smart one over on a Parisian. They'd sit back and wait to see him do it again. That's what I'm waiting for too. He was a lawyer, wasn't he? You don't tell me he hasn't managed somehow to make those papers just rubbish."

"I think," Charlot said, "he was too frightened to think as clearly as that. If he'd thought all that clearly, he'd have died, wouldn't he?"

"When he dies," the girl said, "you can take your oath it will be in a state of grace with the sacrament in his mouth, forgiving all his enemies. He won't die before he can cheat the Devil."

"How you hate him."

"I'll be the one who's damned. Because I shan't forgive. I shan't die in a state of grace." She said, "I

87

thought you were hungry. You didn't eat much of that cheese. It's good cheese."

"It's time I got along," he said.

"You don't have to hurry. Did they let him have a priest?"

"Oh, yes, I think so. They had a priest in one of the other cells who used to do that sort of job."

"Where are you going from here?"

"I don't know."

"Looking for a job?"

"I've given up looking."

She said, "We could do with a man here. A couple of women can't keep a place like this clean. And there's the garden."

"It wouldn't do."

"It's as you like. Wages wouldn't be a difficulty," she said bitterly. "We're rich."

He thought, If only for a week . . . to be quiet . . . at home.

She said, "But your chief job, what I'd be paying you for, is just to keep on looking out—for him."

9

For twenty-four hours it was strange and bitter to be living in his own house as an odd-job man, but after another twenty-four it was familiar and peaceful. If a man loves a place enough he doesn't need to possess it: it's enough for him to know that it is safe and unaltered—or only altered in the natural way by time and circumstance. Madame Mangeot and her daughter were like temporary lodgers. If they took a picture down it was only for some practical purpose—to save dusting, not because they wished to put another in its place; they would never have cut down a tree for the sake of a new view, or refurbished a room according to some craze of the moment. It was exaggeration even to regard them as legal lodgers: they were more like gypsies who had found the house empty and now lived in a few rooms, cultivated a corner of the garden well away from the road, and were careful to make no smoke by which they could be detected.

This was not entirely fanciful: he found they were in fact afraid of the village. Once a week the girl went into Brinac to the market, walking both ways though Charlot knew there was a cart they could have hired in St. Jean, and once a week the old woman went to Mass, her daughter taking her to the door of the church and meeting her there afterwards. The old woman never entered until a few moments before the Gospel was read, and at the very first moment, when the priest had pronounced the *Ita Missa*, she was on her feet. Thus she avoided all contact outside the church with the congregation. This suited Charlot well. It never occurred to either of them as strange that he too should avoid the village.

It was he who now went into Brinac on market day. The first time that he went he felt betrayed at every step by familiar things. It was as though even if no human spoke his name the signpost at the cross-roads would betray him: the soles of his shoes signed his name along the margin of the road, and the slats of the bridge across the river sounded a personal note under his tread which seemed to him as unmistakable as an accent. Once on the road a cart passed him from St. Jean and he recognized the driver—a local farmer who had been crippled as a boy, losing his right arm in an accident with a tractor. As children they had played together in the fields round St. Jean, but after the boy's accident and the long weeks in hospital obscure emotions of jealousy and pride kept them apart, and when they met at last it was as enemies. They couldn't, like duelists, use the same weapons: his own strength was matched against the crippled boy's wounding tongue which bore the bedsores of a long sickness.

Charlot stepped back into the ditch as the cart went by and put up his hand to shield his face, but Roche paid him no attention; the dark fanatical eyes watched the road in front, the great lopped torso stood like a ruined buttress between him and the world. In any case, as Charlot soon realized, there were too many on the roads to attract attention. All over France men were picking their way home, from prison camps, from hiding places, from foreign parts. If one had possessed a God's-eye view of France, one would have detected a constant movement of tiny grains moving like dust across a floor shaped like a map.

He felt an enormous sense of relief when he returned to the house: it was really as if he had emerged from a savage and unaccountable country. He came in at the front door and trod the long passage to the kitchen as though he were retreating into the interstices of a cave. Thérèse Mangeot looked up from the pot she was stirring and said, "It's odd the way you always come in at the front. Why don't you use the back door like we do? It saves a lot of cleaning."

"I'm sorry, mademoiselle," he said. "I suppose it's because I came that way first."

She didn't treat him like a servant: it was as if in her eyes he was just another gypsy camping there until the police turned them out. Only the old woman sometimes fell into an odd apoplectic rage at nothing at all and swore that when her son returned, they would live properly, like the rich people they were, with servants who were really servants, and not tramps taken off the road . . . On these occasions Thérèse Mangeot would turn away as if she didn't hear, but afterwards she would fling some rough inapposite remark to Charlot—the kind of remark you only make to an equal, giving him as it were the freedom of the street.

He said, "There wasn't much to be got in the market. It seemed absurd to be buying so many vegetables with this big garden here. Next year you won't have to . . ." He counted out the money. He said, "I got some horsemeat. There wasn't even a rabbit there. I think the change is right. You'd better check it."

"I'll trust you," she said.

"Your mother won't. Here's my account." He held out to her the list of things he had bought and watched her over her shoulder as she checked. "Jean-Louis Charlot . . ." She stopped reading. "It's strange," she said, and suddenly looking over her shoulder he realized what he had done—he had as near as made no difference signed his name as he had signed it on the deed of gift.

"What's strange?" he asked.

"I could almost swear," she said, "that I knew your writing, that I'd seen it somewhere . . ."

"I suppose you've seen it on a letter I've written."

"You haven't written any letters."

"No. That's true." His lips were dry. He said, "Where do you think you've seen it . . . ?" and waited an age for her answer.

She stared at it and stared at it. "I don't know," she said. "It's like those times when you think you've been in a place before. I don't suppose it means a thing."

10

Nearly every day someone came to the door to beg or to ask for work. The vagrants flowed aimlessly west and south, toward the sun and the sea, as if they believed that on the warm wet margin of France anyone could live. The girl gave them money rather than food (it was less scarce), and they drifted on down the weedy path to the river. There was no stability anywhere, least of all in the big house. And yet the Mangeots had a great sense of property. In Paris Madame Mangeot had owned a small general shop—or rather she had owned the goods in the general shop. Year after year, since her husband had died, she had traded carefully—never giving credit and never accepting credit, and never making more than a bare livelihood. Her husband had had ambitions for his children: he had sent his daughter to a secretarial school to learn typewriting and his son to a technical college, but Janvier had run away, and Thérèse had been withdrawn soon after he died. It was all nonsense, that, in Madame Mangeot's eyes, and the sole result of the few months' training was a secondhand typewriter in the back of the shop on which she typed letters—very badly—to wholesalers. There was no future for the store, but Madame Mangeot didn't worry about that. When you reach a certain age you don't care about the future: it is success enough to be alive; every morning you wake with triumph. And there was always Michel. Madame Mangeot believed implicitly in Michel. Who knows what fairy stories of her infancy gathered about the enigmatic absent figure? He was the prince searching the world with a glass slipper; he was the cowherd who won the King's daughter; he was an old woman's youngest son who killed the giant. She was never allowed to know that he was after all just dead. Charlot learned this story slowly, from half-sentences, outbreaks of temper on the part of Madame Mangeot, even from the dreams the two women recounted at breakfast. It wasn't quite the truth, of course—nothing is ever that, and Madame Mangeot's neighbors in Menilmontant would never have recognized this colored version of her commonplace story. Now suddenly she had come into a fortune. It was the complete justification of Madame Mangeot's daydreams, but the stories of her childhood had also warned her that there was such a thing as fairy gold. Without knowing why, she never felt sure of anything in this house, even of the kitchen table or the chair she sat in, as she had felt sure of everything in Menilmontant, where she knew exactly what had been paid for and what hadn't. Here nothing, as far as she knew, had been paid for: she wasn't to realize that the payment had been made elsewhere.

Charlot slept at the top of the house in what had once been the best servant's bedroom—a little room under a sloping roof with an iron bedstead and a flimsy bamboo chest of drawers, the flimsiest thing in the house where every piece of furniture was heavy and dark and built to last generations. This was the only part of the house he hadn't known: as a child he was forbidden the top floor for some obscure maternal reason that seemed vaguely to be based on morality and hygiene. Up there, where the carpet stopped, beyond the region of bathroom and lavatory, the physical facts of life seemed to lurk with a peculiar menace. Once and once only had he penetrated into the forbidden territory: on tiptoe, under the light weight of six years, he had approached the bedroom he now slept in and peeked round the door. The old servant, whom his parents had inherited and whom they called with rather terrified respect Madame Warnier, was doing her hair—or rather she was taking off her hair: great strands of pale brown hair like dry seaweed were unpicked and laid on the dressing table. All over the region lay a sour miasma. For more than a year after he believed that all long hair was like that—detachable.

One night he couldn't sleep: he followed that clandestine track of his childhood the opposite way in search of water. The servants' stairs creaked under his tread, but unlike his footsteps on the way to Brinac they meant nothing: they were new hieroglyphics nobody had learned to read. On the floor below was his own old room: nobody slept in it now, perhaps because it bore too clearly the marks of his occupancy. He went in. It was exactly as he had left it four years before. He pulled open a drawer and there was a ring of stiff collars turning a little yellow like papyrus with disuse. A photograph of his mother stood in a silver frame on his wardrobe. She wore a high whalebone collar and stared out with an expression of complete calm on a scene that never changed: death and torture and loss had no effect on the small patch of wall that met her gaze—the old wallpaper with sprigs of flowers that *her* mother-in-law had ordered. Above one sprig was a small penciled face: at fourteen it had meant someone and something he had forgotten, some vague romantic passion of adolescence, perhaps a love and a pain he had believed would last as long as his life. He turned and saw Thérèse Mangeot watching him from the doorway. Seeing her was like remembering. It was as if he had connected a broken wire and the forgotten voice spoke to him out of thirty years ago.

"What are you doing?" she asked roughly. She wore a thick corded dressing-gown like a man's.

"I couldn't sleep, so I came down for water. And then I thought I heard a rat in this room."

"Oh, no, there hasn't been a rat here for four years."

"Why don't you clear out all these things?"

Her dressing-gown cord trailed wearily across the floor. "It would almost make one sick, wouldn't it," she said, "to touch them? But I would all the same.

Even the collars." She sat down on the bed: it seemed to Charlot inexpressibly sad that anyone so young should be so tired—and yet awake. "Poor thing," she said.

"Wouldn't it be better if she knew?"

"I didn't mean my mother. I mean her—in the photograph. It can't have been much to boast about, can it, being his mother?"

For the first time since his arrival he found himself stung into protest. "I think you're wrong. I knew him, after all, and you didn't. Believe me—he wasn't such a bad chap."

"Good God," she said.

"He acted like a coward, of course, but, after all, anybody's liable to play the coward once. Most of us do and forget about it. It was just that the once in his case proved—well, so spectacular."

She said, "You can't tell me he was unlucky. It's as you say. That thing happens to everyone once. All one's life one has to think: Today it may happen." It was obvious that she had brooded and brooded on this subject, and now at last she brought out the result aloud for anyone's hearing. "When it happens you know what you've been all your life."

He had no answer: it seemed to him quite true. He asked her sourly, "Has it happened to you yet?"

"Not yet. But it will."

"So you don't know what you are. Perhaps you are no better than he is." He picked up a yellow collar and twirled it angrily and trivially round his wrist.

"That doesn't make him any better," she said,

"does it? If I'm a murderer, must I pretend that other murderers . . . ?"

He interrupted her, "You've got an answer, haven't you, to everything? If you were a man you'd make a good lawyer. Only you'd be a better counsel for the prosecution than for the defense."

"I wouldn't want to be a lawyer," she told him seriously. "He was one."

"How you hate him."

"I've got such hate," she said, "it goes on and on all day and all night. It's like a smell you can't get rid of when something's died under the floorboards. You know that I don't go to Mass now. I just leave my mother there and come back. She wanted to know why, so I told her I'd lost my faith. That's a little thing that can happen to anyone, can't it? God wouldn't pay much account to anyone losing faith. That's just stupidity and stupidity's good." She was crying but from her eyes only: it was as if she had everything under control except the mere mechanism of the ducts. "I wouldn't mind a thing like that. But it's the hate that keeps me away. Some people can drop their hate for an hour and pick it up again at the church door. I can't. I wish I could." She put her hands over her eyes as if she was ashamed of this physical display of grief. He thought, This is all my work.

"You're one of the unlucky ones who believe," he said gloomily.

She got up from the bed. "What's the good of talking? I'd like him here in front of me and me with a gun."

"Have you got a gun?"

"Yes."

"And afterwards I suppose you'd go to confession and be happy again."

"Perhaps. I don't know. I can't think so far."

He said, "You good ones are so horrifying. You get rid of your hate like a man gets rid of his lust."

"I wish I could. I'd sleep better. I wouldn't be so tried and old." She added in a serious voice, "People would like me. I wouldn't be afraid of them any more."

He felt he was in front of a ruin: not an old ruin which has gained the patina and grace of age, but a new ruin where the wallpaper crudely hangs and the wound lies rawly open to show a fireplace and a chair. He thought to himself, It isn't fair. This isn't my fault. I didn't ask for two lives—only Janvier's.

"You can have those collars," she said, "if they are any good to you. Only don't let Mother know. Do they fit you?"

He replied with habitual caution, "Near enough."

"I'll get you a glass of water."

"Why should you get me the water? I'm the servant here."

"The Mangeots," she said, "don't run to servants. Anyway I want to walk about a bit. I can't sleep."

She went away and came back holding the glass. As she stood there in the rough dressing-gown holding the glass out to him he instinctively recognized the meaning of her action. She had told him all about her hate and now she wanted to indicate by a small gesture of service that she had other capacities. She could be a friend, she seemed to indicate, and she could be gentle.

That night, lying in bed, he felt a different quality in his despair. He no longer despaired of a livelihood: he despaired of life.

11

When he woke the details of the scene, even the details of his emotions, had blurred. Everything for a while might have been the same as before, but when he put his hand on the knob of the kitchen door and heard her stirring within, his troubled heart beat out an unmistakable message under his ribs. He walked straight out of the house to try to clear his thoughts, and over the small patch of cultivated garden he spoke aloud the fact, "I love her," across the cabbages as if it were the first statement of a complicated case. But this was a case of which he couldn't see the end.

He thought, Where do we go from here? And his lawyer's mind began to unpick the threads of the case, and to feel some encouragement. In all his legal experience there had never been a case which didn't contain an element of hope. After all, he argued, only Janvier is responsible for Janvier's death: no guilt attaches to me whatever I may feel—one mustn't go by feeling or many an innocent man would be guillotined. There was no reason in law, he told himself, why he should not love her, no reason except her hate why

she should not love him. If he could substitute love for
hate, he told himself with exquisite casuistry, he would
be doing her a service which would compensate for
anything. In her naïve belief, after all, he would be
giving her back the possibility of salvation. He picked
up a pebble and aimed it at a distant cabbage: it
swerved unerringly to its mark, and he gave a little
satisfied sigh. Already the charge against himself had
been reduced to a civil case in which he could argue
the terms of compensation. He wondered why last
night he had despaired—this was no occasion for despair, he told himself, but for hope. He had something
to live for, but somewhere at the back of his mind the
shadow remained, like a piece of evidence he had deliberately not confided to the court.

With their coffee and bread, which they took
early because it was market day at Brinac, Madame
Mangeot was more difficult than usual: she had now
accepted his presence in the house, but she had begun
to treat him as she imagined a great lady would treat
a servant and she resented his presence at their meals.
She had got it firmly into her head that he had been a
manservant to Michel, and that one day her son would
return and be ashamed of her for failing to adapt herself to riches. Charlot didn't care: he and Thérèse
Mangeot shared a secret. When he caught her eye he
believed that they were recalling to each other a secret
intimacy.

But when they were alone he only said, "Can I
find you anything at the market? For yourself, I
mean?"

"No," she said. "There's nothing I want. Anyway, what would there be at Brinac?"

"Why don't you come yourself?" he said. "The walk would do you good . . . a bit of air? You never get out."

"Somebody might come when I was away."

"Tell your mother not to open the door. Nobody's going to break in."

"He might come."

"Listen," Charlot earnestly implored her, "you're driving yourself crazy. You're imagining things. Why, in heaven's name, should he come *here* to be tormented by the sight of everything he's signed away? You're making yourself ill with a dream."

Reluctantly she lifted up one corner of her fear like a child exposing the broken crinkled edge of a transfer. "They don't like me in the village," she said. "They like him."

"We aren't going to the village."

She took him by surprise at the suddenness and completeness of her capitulation. "Oh," she said, "all right. Have it your own way. I'll come."

An autumn mist moved slowly upward from the river. The slats of the bridge were damp beneath their feet, and brown leaves lay in drifts across the road. Shapes faded out a hundred yards ahead. For all the two of them knew they were one part of a long scattered procession on the way to Brinac market, but they were as alone on this strip of road between the two mists as in a room. For a long while they didn't speak: only their feet moving in and out of step indulged in a kind of broken colloquy. His feet moved steadily toward their end like a lawyer's argument: hers were uneven like a succession of interjections. It occurred to him how closely life was imitating the kind of future he had once the right to expect, and yet how distantly. If he had married and brought his wife to St. Jean, they too might in just this way have been walking silently together into the market on a fine autumn day. The road rose a few feet and carried them momentarily out of the mist. A long gray field stretched on either side of them, flints gleaming like particles of ice, and a bird rose and flapped away; then again they moved downhill between their damp insubstantial walls, and his footsteps continued the steady unanswerable argument.

"Tired?" he asked.

"No."

"It's still strange for me to be walking on and on in a straight line, instead of up and down."

She made no reply and her silence pleased him: nothing was more intimate than silence, and he had the feeling that if they remained quiet long enough everything would be settled between them.

They didn't speak again until they were nearly in Brinac. "Let's rest a little," he said, "before we go in." Leaning against a gate they took the weight off their legs and heard the clip-clop of a cart coming down the road from the direction of St. Jean.

It was Roche. He checked his pony and the cart drew slowly up beside them.

"Want a lift?" he asked. He had developed a habit of keeping himself in profile, so as to hide his

102

right side, and it gave him an air of arrogance, a "take it or leave it" manner. Thérèse Mangeot shook her head.

"You're Mademoiselle Mangeot, aren't you?" he asked. "You don't need to walk into Brinac."

"I wanted to walk."

"Who's this?" Roche said. "Your man-of-all-work? We've heard about him in St. Jean."

"He's a friend of mine."

"You Parisians ought to be careful," Roche said. "You don't know the country. There are a lot of beggars about now who are better left begging."

"How you gossip in the country," Thérèse Mangeot said sullenly.

"And you," Roche addressed Charlot, "you are very quiet. Haven't you anything to say for yourself? Are you a Parisian too?"

"One would think," Thérèse Mangeot said, "that you were a policeman."

"I'm of the Resistance," Roche replied. "It's my business to keep an eye on things."

"The war's over for us, isn't it? You haven't any more to do."

"Don't you believe it. It's just beginning down here. You'd better show me your papers," he said to Charlot.

"And if I don't?"

"Some of us will call on you at the house."

"Show them to him," Thérèse Mangeot said.

Roche had to drop the reins to take them, and the pony, released, moved a little way down the road. Suddenly he looked odd and powerless like a boy who has been left in charge of a horse he can't control. "Here," he said, "take them back," and snatched the reins.

"I'll hold the pony for you if you like," Charlot offered with studied insulting kindness.

"You'd better get proper papers. These aren't legal." He turned his face to Thérèse Mangeot. "You want to be careful. There are a lot of queer fish about these days, hiding, most of them. I've seen this fellow somewhere before, I'll swear to that."

"He markets every week. You've probably seen him there."

"I don't know."

Thérèse Mangeot said, "You don't want to raise trouble. The man's all right. I know he's been in a German prison. He knew Michel."

"Then he knew Chavel too?"

"Yes."

Roche peered at him again. "It's odd," he said. "That's why I thought I knew him. He's a bit like Chavel himself. It's the voice: the face of course is quite different."

Charlot said slowly, wondering which syllable betrayed him: "You wouldn't think my voice was like his if you could hear him now. He's like an old man. He took prison hard."

"He would. He'd lived soft."

"I suppose you were his friend," Thérèse Mangeot said. "They all are in St. Jean."

"You suppose wrong. You couldn't know him well and be his friend. Even when he was a boy he was

a mean little squit. No courage. Afraid of the girls."
He laughed. "He used to confide in me. He thought I
was his friend until I had this accident. He couldn't
stand me after that because I'd grown as wise as he
thought he was. If you are in bed for months you
grow wise or die. But the things he used to tell me. I
can remember some of them now. There was a girl at
Brinac mill he was sweet on . . ."

It was extraordinary what things one could forget. Was that the face, he wondered, that he had
drawn so inexpertly on the wallpaper? He could remember nothing, and yet once— "Oh, she was everything to him," Roche said, "but he never dared speak
to her. He was fourteen or fifteen then. A coward if
ever there was one."

"Why do they like him there in the village?"

"Oh, they don't like him," Roche said. "It's just
they didn't believe your story. They couldn't believe
anyone would die for money like your brother did.
They thought the Germans must be mixed up in it
somehow." His dark fanatic eyes brooded on her. "I
believe it all right. It was you he was thinking about."

"I wish you'd convince them."

"Have they troubled you?" Roche asked.

"I don't suppose it's a case of what you call
trouble. I tried to be friendly, but I didn't like being
shouted at. They were afraid to do it themselves, but
they taught their children . . ."

"People are suspicious around here."

"Just because one comes from Paris one isn't a
collaborator."

"You ought to have come to me," Roche said.

She turned to Charlot and said, "We didn't know the great man existed, did we?"

Roche laid his whip to the pony's flank and the cart moved away: as it receded the lopped arm came into view—the sleeve sewn up above the elbow, the stump like a bludgeon of wood.

Charlot rebuked her gently: "Now you've made another enemy."

"He's not so bad," she said, looking after the cart for so long a time that Charlot felt the first septic prick of jealousy.

"You'd better be careful of him."

"You say that just as if you knew him. You don't know him, do you? He seemed to think he'd seen you . . ."

He interrupted her: "I know his type, that's all."

12

That night, after they had returned from Brinac, Thérèse Mangeot behaved in an unaccustomed way— she insisted that they should eat in future in the dining room instead of in the kitchen where previously they had taken all their meals, hurriedly as if they were prepared at any moment for the real owner of the house to appear and claim his rights again. What made the change Charlot had no means of knowing, but his thoughts connected the change with the meeting on the Brinac road. Perhaps the farmer's attack on Chavel had given her confidence, the idea that one man at any

106

rate in St. Jean was prepared to play her friend against him.

Charlot said, "It'll need sweeping out," and took a broom. He was making for the stairs when the girl stopped him.

She said, "We've never used the room before."

"No?"

"I've kept it locked. It's the kind of room he'd have swaggered in. It's smart. Can't you imagine him drinking his wine and ringing for his servants?"

"You sound like a romantic novel," he said and moved to the foot of the stairs.

"Where are you going?"

"To give the room the once-over of course."

"But how do you know where it is?" It was like putting his foot on a step that didn't exist: he felt his heart lurching with the shock; for days he had been so careful, pretending ignorance of every detail, the position of every room or cupboard.

"What am I thinking of?" he said. "Of course. I was listening to you."

But she wasn't satisfied. She watched him closely. She said, "I sometimes think you know this house far better than I do."

"I've been in this sort of house before. They follow a pattern."

"Do you know what I've been thinking? That perhaps Chavel used to boast about his house in prison, draw pictures of it even, until you got to know . . ."

"He talked a lot," he said.

She opened the door of the dining room and they went in together. The room was shuttered and in

107

darkness, but he knew where to turn on the light. He was cautious now and shuffled a long time before he found the switch. It was the biggest room in the house with a long table under a dust sheet standing like a catafalque in the center, and portraits of dead Chavels hanging a little askew. The Chavels had been lawyers since the seventeenth century with the exception of a few younger sons in the church; a bishop with a long twisted nose hung between the windows, and the long nose followed them round from wall to wall, portrait to portrait.

"What a set," she commented. "Maybe he hardly had a chance to turn out differently."

He turned his own long nose up to the face of his grandfather and the man in robes stared down at the man in the green baize apron. He looked away from the supercilious accusing eyes.

"What a set," the girl said again. "And yet they married and had children. Can you imagine them in love?"

"That happens to anyone."

She laughed. It was the first time he had heard her laugh. He watched her avidly, just as a murderer might wait with desperate hope for a sign of life to return and prove him not after all guilty.

She asked, "How do you think they'd show a thing like that? Would they blow those long noses? Do you think they could weep out of those lawyers' eyes?"

He put out a hand and touched her arm. He said, "I expect they'd show it in this way . . ." and at that

108

moment the front doorbell began to clatter and clang on its long metal stalk.

"Roche?" he wondered.

"What would he want?"

"It's too late for beggars, surely?"

"Perhaps," she said breathlessly, "it's him at last."

Again they could hear the long steel tendril quiver before the bell shook. "Open it," she said, "or my mother will come."

He was gripped by the apprehension anyone feels at any time hearing a bell ring at night. He moved uneasily down the stairs with his eyes on the door. So much experience and so much history had contributed to that ancestral fear: murders a hundred years old, stories of revolution and war . . . Again the bell rang as if the man outside were desperately anxious to enter, or else had a right to demand admittance. The fugitive and the pursuer give the same ring.

Charlot put up the chain and opened the door a few inches only. He could see nothing in the dark outside except the faint glimmer of a collarband. A foot stirred on the gravel and he felt the door strain under a steady pressure against the chain. He asked, "Who's that?" and the stranger replied in accents inexplicably familiar, "Jean-Louis Chavel."

Part Three

13

"Who?"

"Chavel." The voice gained confidence and command. "Would you mind opening the door, my good fellow, and letting me in?"

"Who is it?" the girl said: she had paused halfway down the stairs.

A wild hope beat in Charlot's breast, and he called to her in fearful hilarity and relief, "Chavel. He says he's Chavel." Now, he thought, at last I am really Charlot. Somebody else can bear all the hate . . .

"Let him in," she said, and he unchained the door.

The man who came in was as familiar as the voice, but Charlot couldn't place him. He was tall and well made with an odd effect of vulgarity that came from a certain flashiness, something almost jaunty in his walk . . . His skin was very white and looked powdered, and when he spoke his voice was like that of a singer: he seemed too aware of its intonations. You felt he could play any tune on it he pleased.

"My dear lady," he said, "you must excuse my

breaking in like this." His gaze passed to Charlot and he suddenly paused: it was as though he too recognized . . . or thought he recognized . . .

"What do you want?" Thérèse said.

He dragged his eyes reluctantly from Charlot and said, "Shelter—and a bit of food."

Thérèse said, "And you are really Chavel?"

He said uncertainly, "Yes, yes, I am Chavel."

She came down the stairs and across the hall to him. She said, "I thought you'd come . . . one day."

He put his hand out as though his mind couldn't grasp the possibility of anything beyond the conventional. "Dear lady," he said, and she spat full in his face. This was what she had looked forward to all these months, and now it was over, like a child at the end of a party, she began to cry.

"Why don't you go?" Charlot said.

The man who called himself Chavel was wiping his face with his sleeve. He said, "I can't. They are looking for me."

"Why?"

He said, "Anybody who has an enemy anywhere is a collaborationist."

"But you were in a German prison."

"They say I was put there as an informer," the man said quietly. The promptitude of the retort seemed to give him back his self-respect and confidence. He said to the girl slowly, "Of course. You are Mademoiselle Mangeot. It was wrong of me to come here, I know, but any hunted animal makes for the earth it knows. You must forgive my want of tact, mademoiselle. I'll go at once."

She sat on the bottom step of the stairs with her face covered by her hands.

"Yes, you'd better go quickly," Charlot said.

The man swiveled his white powdery face around on Charlot. His lips were dry and he moistened them with a tiny bit of tongue; the only genuine thing about him was his fear. But the fear was under control: like a vicious horse beneath a good rider it showed only in the mouth and the eyeball. He said, "My only excuse is that I had a message for mademoiselle from her brother." Charlot's unremitting, curious gaze seemed to disconcert him. He said, "I seem to know you."

The girl looked quickly up. "You ought to know him. He was in the same prison."

Again Charlot had to admire the man's control.

"Ah, I think it comes back," the man said, "there were a great many of us."

"Is he really Chavel?" the girl asked.

The fear was still there, but it was hidden firmly and Charlot was amazed at the man's effrontery. The white face turned like a naked globe toward him prepared to outglance him, and it was Charlot who looked away. "Yes," he said, "it's Chavel. But he's changed." An expression of glee crinkled the man's face and then all was smooth again.

"Well," the girl asked, "what's your message?"

"It was just that he loved you and this was the best thing he could do for you."

It was bitterly cold in the big hall, and the man suddenly shivered. He said, "Goodnight, mademoiselle. Forgive my intrusion. I should have known that the earth is closed." He bowed with stagy grace, but the gesture was lost on her. She had turned her back on him and was already passing out of sight round a turn of the stairs.

"The door, Monsieur Chavel," Charlot mocked him.

But the man had one shot left. "You are an imposter," he said. "You were not in the prison, you did not recognize me. Do you think I would have forgotten any face there? I think I ought to expose you to your mistress. You are obviously preying on her good nature."

Charlot let him ramble on, plunging deeper. Then he said, "I was in the prison and I did recognize you, Monsieur Carosse."

"Good God," he said, taking the longest look he had yet. "Not Pidot? It can't be Pidot with that voice."

"No, you mistook me for Pidot once before. My name is Charlot. This is the second time you've done me a service, Monsieur Carosse."

"You give me a poor return then, don't you, pushing me out into the night like this? The wind's east, and I'm damned if it hasn't begun to rain." The more afraid he was, the more jaunty he became: jauntiness was like a medicine he took for the nerves. He turned up the collar of his overcoat. "To be given the bird in the provinces," he said, "a poor end to a distinguished career. Good night, my ungrateful Charlot. How did I ever mistake you for poor Pidot?"

"You'll freeze."

"Only too probable. So did Edgar Allan Poe."

"Listen," Charlot said, "I'm not as ungrateful as

that. You can stay one night. Take off your shoes while I slam the door." He closed the door loudly. "Follow me."

But he had only taken two steps when the girl called from the landing, "Charlot, has he gone?"

"Yes, he's gone." He waited a moment and then called up, "I'll make sure the back door is closed," and then he led the man in his stockinged feet down the passage leading to the kitchen quarters, up the back stairs, to his own room.

"You can sleep here," he said, "and I'll let you out early tomorrow. Nobody must see you go, or I shall have to go with you." The man sat comfortably on the bed and stretched his legs. "Are you *the* Carosse?" Charlot asked curiously.

"I know no other Carosse but myself," the man said. "I have no brothers, no sisters, and no parents. I wouldn't know if somewhere in the wastes of the provinces live a few obscure Carosses; there may be a second cousin in Limoges. Of course"—he winced slightly—"there is still my first wife, the old bitch."

"And now they are after you?"

"There is an absurd puritanical conception abroad in this country," Monsieur Carosse said, "that man can live by bread alone. A most un-Catholic idea. I suppose I could have lived on bread—black bread—during the occupation, but the spirit requires its luxuries." He smiled confidently. "One could only obtain luxuries from one source."

"But what induced you to come here?"

"The police, my dear fellow, and these ardent young men with guns who call themselves the Resistance. I was aiming south, but unfortunately my features are too well-known, except," he said with a touch of bitterness, "in this house."

"But how did you know . . . what made you think . . . ?"

"Even in classical comedy, my friend, one becomes accustomed to gag." He smoothed his trousers. "This was a gag, but not, you will say, my most successful. And yet, you know, had I been given time I would have played her in," he said with relish.

"I still don't know how you came here."

"Just an impromptu. I was in an inn about sixty miles from here, a place beginning, I think, with B. I can't remember its name. A funny old boy who had been released from prison was drinking there with his cronies. He was quite a person in the place, the mayor, I gathered—you know the sort, with a paunch and a fob and a big watch the size of a cheese and enormous pomposity. He was telling them the whole story of this man who bought his life, the tenth man he called him: quite a good title, that. He had some grudge against him, I couldn't understand what. Well, it seemed to me unlikely that this Chavel would ever have had the nerve to go home—so I decided to go home for him. I could play the part much better than he could—a dull lawyer type, but of course *you* know the man."

"Yes, you hadn't counted on that."

"Who would? The coincidence is really too great. You *were* in the prison, I suppose? You aren't playing the provinces too?"

"No, I was there."

118

"Then why did you pretend to recognize me?"

Charlot said, "She's always had the idea that Chavel would turn up one day. It's been an obsession. I thought you might cure that obsession. Perhaps you have. I'll have to go now. Unless you want to be turned out into the rain, don't move from here."

He found Thérèse back in the dining room. She was staring at the portrait of his grandfather. "There's no likeness," she said, "no likeness at all."

"Don't you think perhaps in the eyes . . ."

"No, I can't see any. You're more like that painting than he is."

He said, "Shall I lay the table now?"

"Oh, no," she said, "we can't have it in here now that he's around."

"There's nothing to be afraid of. You see, the transfer's genuine. He'll never trouble you any more." He said, "You can forget all about him now."

"That's just what I can't do. Oh," she broke out passionately, "you can see what a coward I am. I said the other day that everyone's tested once and afterwards you know what you are. Well, I know now all right. I ought to shake him by the hand and say 'Welcome, brother: we're both of the same blood.'"

"I don't understand," Charlot said. "You turned him out. What more could you have done?"

"I could have shot him. I always told myself I'd shoot him."

"You can't walk away and fetch a gun and come back and shoot a man in cold blood."

"Why not? He had my brother shot in cold blood. There must have been plenty of cold blood, mustn't there, all through the night? You told me they shot him in the morning."

Again he was stung into defense. "There was one thing I didn't tell you. Once during the night he tried to call the deal off. And your brother would have none of it."

"Once," she said, "once. Fancy that. He tried once. I bet he tried hard."

They had supper as usual in the kitchen. Madame Mangeot asked peevishly what the noise had been in the hall. "It was like a public meeting," she said.

"Only a beggar," Charlot said, "who wanted to stay the night."

"Why did you let him into the house? Such riff-raff we get here when my back's turned. I don't know what Michel would say."

"He didn't get beyond the hall, Mother," Thérèse said.

"But I heard two of them go along the passage toward the kitchen. It wasn't you. You were up-stairs."

Charlot said quickly, "I couldn't turn him out without so much as a piece of bread. That wouldn't have been human. I let him out the back way." Thérèse somberly looked away from him, watching the wet world outside. They could hear the rain coming up in gusts against the house, beating against the windows and dripping from the eaves. It wasn't a night for any human being to be abroad in, and he thought, how she must hate Chavel. He thought of Chavel detachedly as another man: he had been enabled to lose his identity, he thought, forever.

It was a silent meal. When it was over Madame Mangeot lumbered straight off to bed. She never helped in the house now, nor would she wait to see her daughter working. What she didn't see she didn't know. The Mangeots were landowners: they didn't work, they hired others . . .

"He didn't look a coward," Thérèse said.

"You can forget him now."

"That rain's following him," Thérèse said. "All the way from this house it's followed him. That particular rain. It's like a link."

"You needn't think about him any more."

"And Michel's dead. He's really dead now." She passed her palm across the window to wipe away the steam. "Now he's come and he's gone again, and Michel's dead. Nobody else knew him."

"I knew him."

"Oh, yes," she said vaguely. It seemed to be a knowledge that didn't count.

"Thérèse," he said. It was the first time he had called her by that name.

"Yes?" she asked.

He was a conventional man; nothing affected that. His life provided models for behavior in any likely circumstance: they stood around him like tailor's dummies. There had been no model for a man condemned to death, but he had not grown to middle age without making more than one proposal of marriage. The circumstances, however, had been easier. He had been able to state in fairly exact figures the annual amount of his income and the condition of his property. He had been able before that to establish an

121

atmosphere of the right intimacy, and he had been
fairly certain that he and the young woman thought
alike on such things as politics, religion and family life.
Now he saw himself reflected in a canister, carrying
a dishcloth; he was without money, property or pos-
sessions, and he knew nothing of the woman—except
this blind desire of heart and body, this extraordinary
tenderness, a longing he had never experienced before
to protect . . .

"What is it?" she said. She was still turned to the
window as though she couldn't dissociate herself from
the long, wet tramp of the pseudo-Chavel.

He said stiffly, "I've been here more than two
weeks. You don't know anything about me."

"That's all right," she said.

"Have you thought what you'll do when she
dies?"

"I don't know. There's time enough to think."
She took her eyes reluctantly away from the streaming
pane. "Maybe I'll marry," she said and smiled at him.

A feeling of sickness and despair took him. There
was no reason after all for him to assume that she had
not left a man behind her in Paris, some stupid boy
probably of her own class who shared her *gamin*
knowledge of the streets round Menilmontant.

"Who?"

"How do I know?" she said lightly. "There aren't
many around here, are there? Roche, the one-armed
hero: I don't much fancy marrying a piece of a man.
There's you, of course . . ."

He found his mouth was dry: it was absurd to
experience this excitement before asking a trades-

woman's daughter . . . but he had missed the opportunity before he could get his tongue to move.
"Maybe," she said, "I'll have to go to Brinac market
for one. I always heard that when you were rich, there
were lots of fortune hunters around. I can't see any
about here."

He began formally again, "Thérèse." He paused,
"Who's that?"

"Only my mother," she said. "Who else could it
be?"

"Thérèse," a voice called from the stairs. "Thérèse."

"You'll have to finish washing up without me,"
Thérèse said. "I know that voice. It's her praying
voice. She won't sleep now till we've done a rosary at
least. Goodnight, Monsieur Charlot." That was what
she always formally called him at the day's end to heal
any wound to his pride the day might have brought.
The moment had gone, and he knew it might be weeks
before it returned. Tonight he had felt certain she was
in the giving mood. Tomorrow . . .

When he opened the door of his room Carosse
was stretched on the bed with his coat draped over
him for warmth; his mouth was open a crack and he
snored irregularly. The click of the latch woke him:
he didn't move, he simply opened his eyes and watched
Charlot with a faint and patronizing smile. "Well," he
asked, "have you all talked me over?"

"For an experienced actor you certainly chose the
wrong part this time."

"I'm not so sure," Carosse said. He sat up in bed
and stroked his broad plump actor's chin. "You know,

I think I was too hasty. I shouldn't have gone away like that. After all, you can't deny that I had aroused interest. That's half the battle, my dear fellow."

"She hates Chavel."

"But then I'm not the real Chavel. You must remember that. I am the idealized Chavel—a Chavel recreated by art. Don't you see what I gain by being untrammeled by the dull and undoubtedly sordid truth? Give me time, my dear chap, and I'd make her love Chavel. You never by any chance saw my Pierre Louchard?"

"No."

"A grand part. I was a drunken worthless roué—a seducer of the worst type. But how the women loved me. I had more invitations from that part alone . . ."

"She spat in your face."

"My dear fellow, don't I know it? It was superb. It was one of the grandest moments I have ever experienced. You can never get quite that realism on the stage. And I think I did pretty well too. The sleeve: what dignity! I bet you she's thinking in her bed tonight of that gesture."

"Certainly," Charlot said, "Chavel can't compete with you."

"I'm always forgetting you knew the man. Can you give me any wrinkle for the part?"

"There's no point in that. You're going before it's light. The curtain's down. May I have my bed, please?"

"There's room enough for two," the actor said, shifting a few inches toward the wall. In tribulation he seemed to be reverting, with hilarity and relief, to the squalor, the vulgarity of his youth. He was no longer the great and middle-aged Carosse. You could almost see youth creep into the veins under the layers of fat. He hitched himself up on an elbow and said slyly, "You mustn't mind what I say."

"What do you mean?"

"Why, my dear fellow, I can see with half an eye that you are in the throes of the tender passion." He belched slightly, grinning across the bed.

"You are talking nonsense," Charlot said.

"It's only reasonable. Here you are, a man at the sexual age when the emotions are most easily stirred by the sight of youth, living alone in the house with a quite attractive young girl—though perhaps a little coarse. Add to that you have been a long time in prison—and knew her brother. It's just a chemical formula, my dear fellow." He belched again. "Food always does this to me," he explained, "when I eat late. I have to be careful about supper if I am entertaining a little friend. Thank God, that sort of romance dies in a few years, and with older women one can be oneself."

"You'd better go to sleep. I'm waking you early tomorrow."

"I suppose you're planning to marry her?"

Charlot, leaning against the washstand, watched Carosse with dull distaste—watched not only Carosse—a mirror on the wardrobe door reflected both of their images: two middle-aged ruined men discussing a young girl. Never before had he been so aware of his age.

"Do you know," Carosse said, "I'm half regretting

125

that I'm leaving here. I believe I could compete with you—even as Jean-Louis Chavel. You haven't any dash, my dear fellow. You ought to have gone in and won tonight when emotion was in the air—thanks to me."

"I wouldn't want to owe you thanks."

"Why ever not? You've nothing against me. You're forgetting I'm not Chavel." He yawned and stretched. "Oh well, never mind." He settled himself comfortably against the wall. "Turn out the light, there's a good fellow," he said and almost immediately he was asleep.

Charlot sat down on the hard kitchen chair, the only other perch. Wherever he looked there were signs of how completely at home the pseudo-Chavel had made himself. His overcoat hung on the door, and a little pool had collected on the linoleum beneath it; on the chair he had hung his jacket. When Charlot shifted he could feel the sagging weight of the other's pocket against his thigh. The bed creaked as the actor rolled comfortably toward the center. Charlot turned off the light and again felt the heavily weighted pocket beat against his leg. The rain washed against the window regularly like surf. The exhilaration and the hope died out of the day, he saw his own desires sprawl upon the bed, ugly and middle-aged. We had better both move on, he thought.

He shifted and felt the heavy pocket beside him. The actor rolled onto his back and began to snore softly and persistently. Charlot could just make out his shape like a couple of meal sacks flung down at random. He put his hand into Carosse's pocket and

126

touched the cold butt of a revolver. It wasn't surprising: we had returned to the day of the armed citizen; it was as normal as a sword would have been three hundred years before. Nevertheless, he thought, it would be better in my pocket than his. It was a small old-fashioned revolver; he rotated the chamber with his finger and found five of the six compartments full. The sixth was empty, but when he held it to his nose he smelled the unmistakable odor of a recent discharge. Something like a rat moved on the bed among the meal sacks: it was the actor's arm. He muttered a phrase Charlot couldn't catch, a word like *destin;* he was probably, even in his sleep, playing a part.

Charlot put the revolver in his own pocket. Then again he felt Carosse's jacket: he drew out a small bundle of papers, fastened with a rubber ring. It was too dark to examine them: carefully he opened the door and went into the passage. He left the door ajar for fear of noise and switched on a light. Then he examined the nature of his lucky dip.

It was obvious at once that these were not Carosse's papers. There was a bill made out to a man called Toupard, a bill dated and receipted in Dijon on 30 March 1939 for a set of fish knives: a long time, he thought, to keep a receipt unless one were very careful. But careful Toupard undoubtedly was—there was his photograph on his identity card to prove it: a timid man afraid of being done, scenting a trap on every path. You could see him—Charlot had known dozens like him in the courts—making endless detours throughout his life with the idea of avoiding danger. How was it that now his papers had come into the possession of

Carosse? Charlot thought of the empty chamber in the actor's revolver. Papers nowadays were more valuable than money. The actor had been ready to play impromptu the part of Chavel for the sake of a night's lodging, but could he have hoped to get away with *this* identity? The answer was, of course, that five years work many changes. At the end of a war all our portraits are out of date: the timid man had been given a gun to slay with, and the brave man had found his nerve fail him in the barrage.

He went back to his room and stowed the papers and the gun back in the actor's pocket. He no longer wished to keep the gun. The door behind him shut suddenly with a crack like a shot, and Carosse leapt upon the bed. His eyes opened on Charlot and he cried with anxiety, "Who are you?" but before an answer came he was again as soundly asleep as a child. Why couldn't all those who have killed a man sleep as soundly? Charlot wondered.

14

"Where've you been?" Thérèse said.

He scraped the mud off his shoes with a knife and replied, "In the night I thought I heard someone move by the garden shed. I wanted to make sure."

"Were there any signs?"

"No."

"It may have been Chavel," she said. "I lay awake for hours thinking. It was an awful night to turn a man out in. There we were, my mother and I, praying and praying. And he was outside walking. So many Paternosters," she said. "I couldn't leave out the bit about forgiveness every time or my mother would have spotted something."

"Better to be walking in the rain than shot."

"I don't know. Is it? It depends, doesn't it? When I spat in his face . . ." She paused, and he remembered very clearly the actor lying on the bed boasting of his gesture. She'll be thinking about it, he had said. It was horrifying to realize that a man as false as that could sum up so accurately the mind of someone so true. The other way round, he thought, it doesn't work. Truth doesn't teach you to know your fellow man.

He said, "It's over now. Don't think about it."

"Do you think he got some shelter? He'd have been afraid to ask for it in the village. It wouldn't have done any harm to have let him spend a night here," she accused him. "Why didn't you suggest that? You haven't any reason to hate him."

"It's better just to put him out of mind. You weren't so anxious to forgive him before you'd seen him."

"It's not so easy to hate a face you know," she said, "as a face you just imagine."

He thought, If that's true what a fool I've been.

"After all," she said, "we are more alike than I thought, and when it came to the point I couldn't shoot him. The test floored me just as it floored him!"

"Oh, if you are looking for points like that," he told her, "take me as an example. Aren't I failure enough for you?"

She looked up at him with a terrible lack of interest. "Yes," she said. "Yes. I suppose you are. Michel sent a message by him."

"So he said."

"I don't see why he should have lied about that and not about the big thing. As a matter of fact," she said with an awful simplicity, "he didn't strike me like a man who told lies."

During the night Madame Mangeot had been taken ill. Those large maternal breasts were after all a disguise of weakness: behind them unnoticeably she had crumbled. It was no case for a doctor and in any event there were not enough doctors in these days to cover so obscure a provincial corner as Brinac. The priest was of more importance to the sick woman, and for the first time Charlot penetrated into the dangerous territory of St. Jean. It was too early in the morning for people to be about and he passed nobody on his way to the presbytery. But there his heart drummed on his ribs as he rang. He had known the old man well: he had been used to dining at the big house whenever Chavel visited St. Jean. He was not a man who could be put off by a beard and the changes a few years wrought on the face, and Charlot felt a mixture of anxiety and expectation. How strange it would feel to be himself again, if only to one man.

But it was a stranger who replied to his ring: a dark youngish man with the brusque air of a competent and hardworking craftsman. He packed the sacrament in his bag as a plumber packs his tools. "Is it wet across the fields?" he asked.

"Yes."

"Then you must wait till I put on my galoshes."

He walked quickly and Charlot had difficulty in maintaining the pace. Ahead of him the galoshes sucked and spat. Charlot said, "There used to be a Father Russe here?"

"He died," the young priest said, striding on, "last year." He added somberly, "He got his feet wet." He added, "You would be surprised at the number of parish priests who die that way. You might call it a professional risk."

"He was a good man, they say."

"It isn't difficult," Father Russe's successor said with asperity, "to satisfy country people. Any priest who has been in a place forty years is a good old man." He sounded as though he sucked his teeth between every word, but it was really his galoshes drawing at the ground.

Thèrése met them at the door. Carrying his little attaché case the priest followed her upstairs: a man with his tools. He could have wasted no time: ten minutes had not passed before he was back in the hall drawing on his galoshes again. Charlot watched from the passage his brisk and businesslike farewell. "If you need me," he said, "send for me again, but please remember, mademoiselle, that though I am at your service I am also at the service of everyone in St. Jean."

"Can I have your blessing, Father?"

"Of course." He rubber-stamped the air like a notary and was gone. They were alone together, and Charlot had never felt their loneliness so complete. It was as if the death had already occurred, and they were left face to face with the situation.

131

Part Four

15

The great actor Carosse sat in the potting shed and considered his situation. He was not cast down by his somewhat humiliating circumstances. He had the democratic feeling of a duke who feels himself safely outside questions of class and convention. Carosse had acted before George V of Great Britain, King Carol of Rumania, the Archduke Otto, the special envoy of the President of the United States, Field Marshal Goering, innumerable ambassadors, including the Italian, the Russian and Herr Abetz. They glittered in his memory like jewels: he felt that one or another of these great or royal men could always when necessary be pawned in return for "the ready." All the same he had been momentarily disquieted early that morning in St. Jean, seeing side by side on the police station wall a poster that included his name in a list of collaborators at large and an announcement of a murder in a village more than fifty miles away. The details of the crime were, of course, unknown to the police, otherwise Carosse felt sure that the description would have read homicide. He had acted purely in self-defense to prevent the foolish little bourgeois from betraying him. He had left the body, he thought, safely concealed under the gorse bushes on the common, and had borrowed the papers which might just get him past a formal cursory examination. Now that they could no longer be useful to him, and might prove dangerous, he had burned them in the potting shed and buried the ashes in a flower pot.

When he saw the two notices he had realized it was no good going further. Not until those notices everywhere had become torn and windblown and discolored by time. He had got to lie up and there was only one house where that was possible. The man Charlot had already lied to his mistress by supporting Carosse's imposture, and he had broken the law by harboring a collaborator: there was evidently here a screw that could be turned sharply. But as he sat on a wheelbarrow and considered the situation further his imagination kindled with a more daring project. In his mind a curtain rose on a romantic situation that only an actor of the finest genius could make plausible, though it was perhaps not quite original: Shakespeare had thought of it first.

Watching through a knothole in the wall he saw Charlot cross the fields toward St. Jean: it was too early for market and he was hurrying. Patiently Carosse waited, his plump backside grooved on the edge of the wheelbarrow, and he saw Charlot return with the priest. Some time later he saw the priest leave alone, carrying his attaché case. His visit could have only one meaning, and immediately the creative process absorbed the new fact and modified the scene he was going to play. But still he waited. If genius be indeed an infinite capacity for taking pains, Carosse was an actor of genius. Presently his patience was rewarded: he saw Charlot leave the house and make his way again toward St. Jean. Brushing the leaf mold off his overcoat Carosse stretched away the cramp like a large, lazy, neutered cat. The gun in his pocket thumped against his thigh.

No actor born has ever quite rid himself of stage fright and Carosse crossing in front of the house to the kitchen door was very frightened. The words of his part seemed to sink out of his mind; his throat dried and when he pulled the bell it was a short timid tiptoe clang that answered from the kitchen, unlike the peremptory summons of his previous visit. He kept his hand on the revolver in his pocket; it was like an assurance of manhood. When the door opened he stammered a little, saying, "Excuse me." But frightened as he was, he recognized that the involuntary stammer had been just right: it was pitiable, and pity had got to wedge the door open like a beggar's foot. The girl was in shadow and he couldn't see her face; he stumbled on, hearing his own voice, how it sounded, and gaining confidence. The door remained open: he didn't ask for anything better yet.

He said, "I hadn't got beyond the village when I heard about your mother. Mademoiselle, I had to come back. I know you hate me but, believe me, I never intended this—to kill your mother too."

"You needn't have come back. She knew nothing about Michel." It was promising; he longed to put his

137

foot across the threshold, but he knew such a move would be fatal. He was a man of cities, unused to country isolation, and he wondered what tradesman might at any moment come up behind his back—or Charlot might return prematurely. He was listening all the time for the scrunch of gravel.

"Mademoiselle," he pleaded, "I had to come back. Last night you didn't let me speak. I didn't even finish the message from Michel." (Damnation, he thought, that's not the part: what message?) He hedged: "He gave it to me the night he died," and was astonished by the success of his speech.

"The night he died? Did he die in the night?"

"Yes, of course. In the night."

"But Charlot told me it was in the morning—the next morning."

"Oh, what a liar that man has always been," Carosse moaned.

"But why should he lie?"

"He wanted to make it worse for me," Carosse improvised. He felt a wave of pride in his own astuteness that carried him over the threshold into the house: Thérèse Mangeot had stepped back to let him in. "It's worse, isn't it, to let a man die after a whole night to think about it? I wasn't villain enough for him."

"He said you tried once to take the offer back."

"Once," Carosse exclaimed. "Yes, once. That was all the chance I had before they fetched him out." The tears stood in his eyes as he pleaded, "Mademoiselle, believe me. It was at night."

"Yes," she said, "I know it was at night. I woke with the pain."

138

"What time was that?"

"Just after midnight."

"That was the time," he said.

"How mean of him," she said. "How mean to lie about that."

"You don't know that man Charlot, mademoiselle, as we knew him in prison. Mademoiselle, I know I'm beneath your contempt. I bought my life at the expense of your brother's, but at least I didn't cheat to save it."

"What do you mean?"

He had remembered the mayor's description of how they all drew lots. He said, "Mademoiselle, we drew in alphabetical order starting at the wrong end because this man Charlot pleaded that it should be that way. At the end there were only two slips left for him and me, and one of them was marked with the death token. There was a draft in the cell and it must have lifted the slips of paper and shown him which was marked. He took out of turn—Charlot should have come after Chavel—and he took the unmarked slip."

She pointed out doubtfully the obvious flaw: "You could have demanded the draw again."

"Mademoiselle," Carosse said, "I thought at the time it was an honest mistake. Where a life depended on it, one couldn't penalize a man for an honest mistake."

"And yet you bought your life?"

He was playing, he knew it, a flawed character. The inconsistencies didn't add up: the audience had to be stormed by romantic acting. He pleaded, "Mademoiselle, there are so many things you don't know.

That man has put the worst light on everything. Your brother was a very sick man."

"I know."

He caught his breath with relief: it was as if now he couldn't go wrong, and he became reckless. "How he loved you and worried about what would happen to you when he died. He used to show me your photograph . . ."

"He had no photograph."

"That astonishes me." It was an understatement: momentarily it staggered him. He had been confident, but he recovered immediately. "There was a photograph he always showed me; it was a street scene torn out of a newspaper—a beautiful girl half hidden in the crowd. I can guess now who it was: it wasn't you, but it seemed to him like you, and so he kept it and pretended . . . People behave strangely in prison, mademoiselle. When he asked me to sell him the slip . . ."

"Oh, no," she said, "no. You are too plausible. He asked *you* . . . That wasn't how it happened."

He told her mournfully, "You have been filled with lies, mademoiselle. I'm guilty enough, but would I have returned if I was as guilty as *he* makes out?"

"It wasn't Charlot. It was the man who sent me the will and the other papers. The Mayor of Bourge."

"You don't have to tell me any more, mademoiselle. Those two men were as thick as thieves. I understand it all now."

"I wish *I* did. I wish I did."

"Between them they cooked it perfectly." With his heart in his mouth, he said, "I will say goodbye,

140

mademoiselle—and God bless you." *Dieu*—he dwelt on the word as though he loved it, and indeed it was a word he loved, perhaps the most effective single word on the romantic stage: "God bless," "I call God to my witness," "God may forgive you"—all the grand hackneyed phrases hung around *Dieu* like drapery. He turned as slowly as he dared toward the door.

"But the message from Michel?"

16

Carosse leaned on the fence gazing toward the small figure that approached across the fields from St. Jean. He leaned like a man taking his ease in his own garden: once he gave a small quiet giggle as a thought struck him, but this was succeeded, as the figure came closer and became recognizably Charlot, by a certain alertness, a tautening of the intelligence.

Charlot, who remembered the revolver in the pocket, stood a little distance away and stared back at him. "I thought you'd gone," he said.

"I decided to stay."

"Here?"

Carosse said gently, "It's my own place, after all."

"Carosse the collaborator?"

"No. Jean-Louis Chavel the coward."

"You've forgotten two things," Charlot said, "if you are going to play Chavel."

"I thought I'd rubbed up the part satisfactorily."

"If you are going to be Chavel you won't be allowed to stay—unless you want more spittle in your face."

"And the other thing?"

"None of this belongs to Chavel any more."

Again Carosse giggled, leaning back from the fence with his hand on the revolver "just in case." He said, "I've got two answers, my dear fellow."

His confidence shook Charlot, who cried angrily across the grass, "Stop acting."

"You see," Carosse said gently, "I've found it quite easy to talk the girl around to my version of things."

"Version of what?"

"Of what happened in the prison. I wasn't there, you see, and that makes it so much easier to be vivid. I'm forgiven, my dear Charlot, but you on the contrary are branded—forgive my laughing, because, of course, I know how grossly unfair it is—as the liar." He gave a happy peal of laughter: it was as if he expected the other to share altruistically his sense of the comedy of things. "You are to clear out, Charlot. Now, at once. She's very angry with you. But I've persuaded her to let you have three hundred francs for wages. That's six hundred you owe me, my dear fellow." And he held out his left hand tentatively.

"And she's letting you stay?" Charlot asked, keeping his distance.

"She hasn't any choice, my dear. She hadn't heard of the Decree of the 17th—nor you either? You don't see the papers here, of course. The decree which makes illegal all change of property that took place during the German occupation if denounced by one

party? Do you really mean to say you never thought
of that? But there, I only thought of it myself this
morning."

Charlot stared back at him with horror. The
fleshy and porky figure of the actor momentarily was
transformed into its own ideal—the carnal and the
proud, leaning negligently there on the axis of the
globe offering him all the kingdoms of the world in
the form of six freehold acres and a house. He could
have everything—or his three hundred francs miracu-
lously renewed. It was as if all that morning he had
moved close to the supernatural: an old woman was
dying and the supernatural closed in. God came into
the house in an attaché case, and when God came the
Enemy was always present. He was God's shadow: he
was the bitter proof of God. The actor's silly laugh
tinkled again, but he heard the ideal laughter swinging
behind, a proud and comradely sound, welcoming him
to the company of the Devil.

"I bet you Chavel thought of it when he signed
the transfer. Oh, what a cunning devil," Carosse giggled with relish. "It's the nineteenth today. I bet he
won't be far behind the decree."

The actual trivial words made no impression on
Charlot's mind. Behind them he heard the Enemy
greeting him like a company commander with ap-
proval—"Well done, Chavel"—and he felt a wave of
happiness: this was home and he owned it. He said,
"What's the good of your pretending to be Chavel
any longer, Carosse? It's as you say. Chavel will be on
his way home."

Carosse said, "I like you, old man. You do remind

143

me of good old Pidot. I'll tell you what—if I pull this
thing off you need never want for a few thousand
francs."

The grass was his and Charlot looked at it with
love. He must have it scythed before winter, and next
year he would take the garden properly in hand . . .
The indentation of footmarks ran up from the river:
he could recognize his own narrow shoe marks and the
wide heavy galoshes of the priest. By this route God
had moved into the house, where it was suddenly as if
the visible world healed and misted and came back
into focus, and he saw Carosse quite clearly again,
porky and triumphant, and he knew exactly what he
had to do. The Decree of the 17th—even the gifts of
the Enemy were gifts also of God. The Enemy was
unable to offer any gift without God simultaneously
offering the great chance of rejection. He asked again,
"But what's the good, Carosse?"

"Why," Carosse said, "even a day's shelter, you
know, is a gain to a man like me. People will come to
their senses soon, and the right ones will get on top.
One just has to keep on hiding." But he couldn't resist
a boast. "But that's not all, my dear man. What a
triumph if I married her before Chavel came. I could
do it. I'm Carosse, aren't I? You know your *Richard
III*. 'Was ever woman in this humour wooed?' And
the answer of course is Yes. Yes, Charlot, yes."

It is always necessary to know one's enemy
through and through. Charlot asked a third time,
"Why? What's the good?"

"I need money, my dear. Chavel can't refuse a

144

split. That would be too abominable after swindling the brother of his life."

"And you think I won't interfere? You said last night that I loved the girl."

"Oh, that!" Carosse breathed the objection away. "You don't love her enough, my dear man, to injure your own chances. You and I are too old for that kind of love. After all, if Chavel comes back you get nothing, but if I win, well, you know I'm generous." It was quite true: he was generous. His generosity was an integral part of his vulgarity. "And anyway," he added, "what can I do? You've told her I'm Chavel."

"You forget I know who you are: Carosse the collaborationist—and murderer."

The right hand shifted in the pocket: a finger moved where the safety catch should be. "You think I'm that dangerous?"

"Yes." Charlot watched the hand. "And there's another thing—I know where Chavel is."

"Where?"

"He's nearly here. And there's another thing. Look down there across the fields. You see the church?"

"Of course."

"You see the hill behind, a little to the right, divided into fields?"

"Yes."

"In the top right-hand corner there's a man working."

"What about it?"

"You can't tell who he is from this distance, but I

know him. He's a farmer called Roche, and he's the
Resistance leader in St. Jean."

"Well?"

"Suppose I went down there now and up the hill
and told him he'd find Carosse at the big house—not
only Carosse but the murderer of a man called Toupard." For a moment he thought Carosse was going to
fire: an act of recklessness and despair in this exposed
place. The sound would carry right across the valley.

But instead he smiled. "My friend," he said, "we
seem to be inextricably tied together."

"You have no objection then if I return with you
to the house." Charlot approached slowly as one
would approach a chained dog.

"Ah, but the lady may."

"The lady, I feel sure, will take your advice."

The right hand came suddenly and cheerfully out
of the pocket and beat twice on Charlot's back.
"Bravo, bravo," Carosse said. "I made a mistake. We'll
work together. You're a man after my own heart.
Why, with a little skill we'll both have a nibble at the
girl as well as at the money." He passed his arm
through Charlot's and urged him gently homeward.

Once Charlot looked back at the tiny figure of
Roche on the hillside: he remembered the period when
they had not been enemies, before sickness had tipped
Roche's tongue with venom . . . The little figure
turned his back and marched up the field behind the
plow.

Carosse squeezed his right arm. "If this Chavel,"
he said, "is really on his way, we'll make a stand
against him—you and I. And if the worst comes to the

worst, you know I've got my gun." He squeezed his arm again. "You won't forget that, will you?"

"No."

"You'll have to apologize for the lies you've told her. She feels badly about those."

"The lies?"

"That her brother died in the morning."

The sun flashed at him from a window of the house. Charlot lowered his dazzled eyes and thought, What am I to do? What am I trying to do?

17

That night Madame Mangeot died. The priest had again been summoned, and from his room on the top floor Charlot heard the sounds of death going on— the footsteps to and fro, the clink of a glass, a tap running, two voices whispering. His door opened and Carosse looked in. He had moved into what he called his own bedroom, but now he was keeping out of the way of strangers.

He whispered, "Thank God, that's nearly over. It gives me the creeps."

Death is not private: the breath doesn't simply stop in the body and that's the end—whisper, clink, the creak of a board, the gush of water into a sink. Death was like an operation performed urgently without the proper attendants—or like a childbirth. One expected at any moment to hear the wail of the newborn, but what one heard at last was simply silence.

The tap was stopped, the glass was quiet, the boards ceased to creak.

Carosse gave a contented sigh. "It's happened." They listened together like conspirators. He whispered, "This brings it to a head. She'll be wondering what to do. She can't stay here alone."

"I must go and see the priest home," Charlot said.

The priest was pulling on his galoshes in the hall. On the way back through the fields he asked curtly, "You'll be leaving now?"

"Perhaps."

"Either you will have to go, or Mademoiselle Mangeot will have to find a companion from the village."

Charlot was irritated by the man's assumption that human actions were governed incontestably by morality—not even by morality, but by the avoidance of scandal. He said, "It's for Mademoiselle Mangeot to decide."

They stopped at the outskirts of the village. The priest said, "Mademoiselle Mangeot is a young woman very easily swayed. She is very ignorant of life, very simple." He stood like a black exclamation mark against the gray early-morning sky: he had an appearance of enormous arrogance and certainty.

"I wouldn't have said that. She has seen a good deal of life in Paris. She is not a country girl," he added maliciously.

"You don't see more of life," the priest said, "in one place than another. One man in a desert is enough life if you are trained to observe or have a bent for observation. She has no bent."

"She seemed to me to have a great deal of *gamin* wisdom."

"You didn't bother, I imagine," the priest said, "to notice whether it was really wisdom?"

"No."

"Shrewdness often sounds like wisdom, and ignorance often sounds like shrewdness."

"What do you want to say—or do?"

"You are a man of education, monsieur, and you won't retort that this is none of my business. You know that it is my business. But you think because I say you must go or Mademoiselle Mangeot must find a companion that I'm prudish. It is not prudery, monsieur, but a knowledge of human nature which it is difficult to avoid if you sit like we do day after day, listening to men and women telling you what they have done and why. Mademoiselle Mangeot is in a condition now when any woman may do a foolish action. All the emotions have something in common. People are quite aware of the sorrow there always is in lust, but they are not so aware of the lust there is in sorrow. You don't want to take advantage of that, monsieur."

The clock in the ugly church struck. It was half past six: the hour when in prison he had made his only attempt to go back on his bargain; the hour when it had first became possible to make out Janvier's unsleeping eyes. He said, "Trust me, Father. I want nothing but good for Mademoiselle Mangeot," and turned and strode rapidly back toward the house. It was the hour when one saw clearly . . .

The lower rooms were in darkness, but there was

149

a light on the landing, and when he entered the hall, he entered so quietly that neither person heard him. They were poised like players before a camera waiting for the director's word to start. So much sorrow in lust and so much lust in sorrow, the priest had said—it was as if they were bent on exhibiting one half of the truth. He wondered what had just been said or done to slice the line of dissatisfaction on the man's cheek and make the girl lean forward with hunger and tears.

"Why don't you leave me alone?" she implored Carosse.

"Mademoiselle," he cried, "you are alone now— so alone. But you need never be alone again. You've hated me, but that's all over. You needn't worry any more over this and that." He knew the game so well, Charlot thought: the restless playboy knew how to offer what most people wanted more than love— peace. The words flowed like water—the water of Lethe.

"I'm so tired."

"Thérèse," he said, "you can rest now."

He advanced a hand along the banister and laid it on hers: she let it lie. She said, "If I could trust anybody at all. I thought I could trust Charlot, but he lied to me about Michel."

"You can trust me," Carosse said, "because I've told you the worst. I've told you who I am."

"Yes," she said, "I suppose so." He moved toward her beside the banister. It seemed incredible to Charlot that his falsity was not as obvious as a smell of sulphur, but she made no effort to avoid him. When he took her in his arms she let herself go with closed eyes like a suicide. Over her shoulder Carosse became suddenly aware of Charlot standing below. He smiled with triumph and winked a secret message.

"Mademoiselle Mangeot," Charlot said. The girl detached herself and looked down at him with confusion and shame. He realized then how young she was, and how old they both were. He no longer felt the desire at all: only an immeasurable tenderness. The light on the landing was dimming as daylight advanced and she looked in the gray tide like a plain child who had been kept from bed by a party that has gone on too long.

"I didn't know you were here," she said. "How long . . . ?"

Carosse watched him carefully; his right hand shifted from the girl's arm to his pocket. He called cheerily down, "Well, Charlot, my dear fellow, did you see the priest safe home?"

"My name," Charlot said, standing in the hall and addressing his words to Thérèse Mangeot, "is not Charlot. I am Jean-Louis Chavel."

18

Carosse called harshly down, "You're mad," but Chavel went on speaking quietly to the girl. "That man is an actor called Carosse. You've probably heard of him. He's wanted by the police as a collaborationist and the murderer of a man called Toupard."

"You're crazy."

"I don't understand," the girl said. She wiped a damp strand of hair from her forehead. She said, "So many lies. I don't know who's lying. Why did you say you recognized him?"

"Yes, tell us that," Carosse called triumphantly.

"I was afraid to tell you who I was because I knew how much you hated me. When he came I thought here was a chance of losing myself forever. He could have all the hatred."

"What a liar you are," Carosse mocked him over the banister. They stood side by side above him and it occurred to Chavel with horror that perhaps he was too late: perhaps this was not simply the lust of grief that the priest had spoken of, but genuine love which would be as ready to accept Carosse the cheat as it had Chavel the coward. He no longer cared about anything in the world but building an indestructible barrier between them—at whatever risk, he thought, at whatever risk.

Carosse said, "You'd better pick up your bed and walk. You're not wanted here any more."

"This house is Mademoiselle Mangeot's. Let her speak."

"What a cheat you are." Carosse put his hand on the girl's arm and said, "He came to me yesterday and told me that this house was really mine: that some decree or other, I don't know what, had made changes during the occupation illegal. As if I'd take advantage of a quibble like that."

Chavel said, "When I was a boy in this house I had a game I used to play with a friend across the valley."

152

"What on earth are you talking about now?"

"Be patient. You'll find the story interesting. I used to take a torch like this or a candle, or if it was a sunny day a mirror—and I used to flash a message like this through the door here. Sometimes it would be just 'Nothing doing.'"

Carosse said, with a note of anxiety, "What are you doing now?"

"This message always meant: 'Help, the Redskins are here.'"

"Oh," the girl said, "I can't understand all this talk."

"The friend still lives over the valley—even though he's not a friend any more. This is the time he'll be going out to the cows. He'll see this light on and off and he'll know Chavel's back. The Redskins are here, he'll read. No one else would know that message." He saw Carosse's hand tighten in the pocket: it was not enough to prove the man a liar. He could turn even a lie to romantic purposes. There must be the indestructible barrier.

Thérèse said, "You mean that if he comes it will prove you are Chavel?"

"Yes."

"He won't come," Carosse said uneasily.

"If he doesn't come, there are other ways of proving it."

"Who is your friend?" Thérèse said, and he noticed that she said "your friend" as if she were already half convinced.

"The farmer Roche: the head of the Resistance here."

The girl said, "But he's seen you already—on the road to Brinac."

"He didn't look very closely. I am much changed, mademoiselle." He took the torch again and stood in the doorway. He said, "He can't help seeing this. He'll be in the yard now—or the fields."

"Put that torch down," Carosse shrieked at him. It was Chavel's moment of triumph. The pretense was over. The actor was like a man under third degree: the sweat, even in the cold early air, stood on his forehead.

Chavel, watching the pocket, shook his head and his body stiffened against the coming pain.

"Put it down."

"Why?"

"Mademoiselle," Carosse implored, "a man has the right to fight for his life. Tell him to put down the torch or I'll shoot."

"You *are* a murderer then?"

"Mademoiselle," he said with absurd sincerity, "there's a war on." He backed along the banister away from her and taking the revolver from the pocket swiveled it between them: they were joined by the punctuation of the muzzle. "Put the torch down."

In the village a clock began to strike seven. Chavel, with the torch depressed, counted the hour: it was the hour of the cinder track and the blank wall and the other man's death. It seemed to him that he had taken a lot of trouble to delay a recurring occasion. Carosse mistook his hesitation: he became masterful. "Now drop your torch and stand away from the door." But Chavel raised it and flashed it again off and on and off and on again.

154

Carosse fired in quick succession. In his agitation the first bullet went wide, splitting the glass of a picture; at the second the torch fell and lay on the hall floor making a little bright path to the door. Chavel's face creased with pain. He was driven back as though by the buffet of a fist against the wall and then the acuteness of the pain passed: he had had far worse pain from an appendix. When he looked up Carosse was gone and the girl was in front of him.

"Are you hurt?"

"No," he said. "Look at the picture. He missed." The two shots had been too rapid for her to distinguish them. He wanted to get her out of the way before anything ugly happened. He moved a few feet gingerly toward a chair and sat down. In a few moments the stain would soak through. He said, "That's over. He'll never dare come back."

She said, "And you really are Chavel?"

"Yes."

"But that was another lie about the message, wasn't it? You never flashed the same way twice."

"Another lie. Yes," he said. "I wanted him to shoot. He can't come back now. He thinks he's killed me like . . . like . . ." He couldn't remember the other man's name. The heat in the hall seemed to him extraordinary at that early hour; sweat ran like mercury beads across his forehead. He said, "He'll have gone the opposite way from St. Jean. Go down there quickly and get the priest to help you. Roche will be useful. Remember he's the actor Carosse."

She said, "You must be hurt."

"Oh, no. I got a ricochet from the wall. That's all.

It's shocked me a bit. Get me a pencil and paper. I'll be writing a report of this while you fetch the police." She brought him what he wanted and stood puzzled and ill at ease before him. He was afraid he'd faint before she'd gone. He said gently, "You're all right now, aren't you? All the hatred's gone?"

"Yes."

"That's good," he said, "good." There was nothing left of his love—desire had no importance: he felt simply a certain pity, gentleness, and the tenderness one can feel for a stranger's misfortune. "You'll be all right now," he told her. "Just run along," he said with slight impatience, as to a child.

"You're all right?" she asked anxiously.

"Yes. Yes."

Immediately she had gone he began to write: he wanted to tie everything up. His lawyer's instinct wanted to make a neat end. He wished he knew the exact wording of the decree, but it was unlikely to affect the original transfer without a denunciation by one party. This note he was writing now—"I leave everything of which I die possessed . . ."—was merely contributing evidence to prove that he had no intention of denouncing; it had no legal force in itself—he had no witness. The blood from his stomach was running now down his leg. It was as well that the girl was out of the way. The touch of blood cooled his fever like water. He took a quick look round: through the open door the light returned now across the fields; it was oddly satisfactory to die in his own home alone. It was as if one possessed at death only what the eyes took in. Poor Janvier, he thought—the cinder track. He began to sign his name, but before he had quite finished he felt the water of his wound flowing immeasurably: a river, a torrent, a tide of peace.

The paper lay on the floor beside him, scrawled over with almost illegible writing. He never knew that his signature read only Jean-Louis Ch . . . which stood of course as plainly for Charlot as for Chavel. A crowning justice saw to it that he was not troubled. Even a lawyer's meticulous conscience was allowed to rest in peace.